"You may be a good driver, Carter. Maybe you are even an outstanding amateur. But YOU'LL NEVER SURVIVE OUT THERE."

"I must!" I shouted.

Within two minutes I was secured in the machine, had strapped on my helmet, and had popped it into first gear.

"Keep it above 8,000 RPM," Offenbach shouted, as I eased up on the clutch and took off.

My speed was well over 200 miles per hour when LeMaigne went by me, and then I forgot everything else except keeping behind LeMaigne and keeping alive . . .

NICK CARTER IS IT!

"Nick Carter out-Bonds James Bond."
—*Buffalo Evening News*

"Nick Carter is America's #1 espionage agent."
—*Variety*

"Nick Carter is razor-sharp suspense."
—*King Features*

"Nick Carter is extraordinarily big."
—*Bestsellers*

"Nick Carter has attracted an army of addicted readers . . . the books are fast, have plenty of action and just the right degree of sex . . . Nick Carter is the American James Bond, suave, sophisticated, a killer with both the ladies and the enemy."
—*The New York Times*

From The Nick Carter Killmaster Series

**Dedicated to The Men of the
Secret Services of the
United States of America**

A Killmaster Spy Chiller

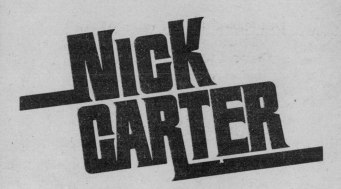

NICK CARTER

RACE OF DEATH

CHARTER
NEW YORK

A DIVISION OF CHARTER COMMUNICATIONS INC.
A GROSSET & DUNLAP COMPANY

RACE OF DEATH

CHARTER BOOKS
A Division of Charter Communications Inc.
A Grosset & Dunlap Company
360 Park Avenue South
New York, New York 10010

Manufactured in the United States of America

I

KAPIOLANI PARK IN in Honolulu is everything the travel brochures say it is, and more. Nothing in print can come even close to describing the beauty of the lush green tropical plants and the deep, almost unreal blue of the sky sharply contrasting with the perfect white of the puffy clouds. Less than five miles away, the majestic crown of Diamond Head, beyond Waikiki Beach, has to be seen to be believed.

But I was bored.

My chief, David Hawk, kingpin in AXE, had set this assignment up for me two weeks ago, and at first I had come back from my rest-and-recuperation leave in Arizona with high hopes for another exciting mission. But that excitement had soon faded to boredom with the full impact of what Hawk had told me.

"You're going to be a bodyguard for the president, Nick," Hawk told me in his office on Dupont Circle of Amalgamated Press—AXE's front organization in Washington, D.C.

"What!" I said, coming forward in my chair. "Bodyguard? Jesus, he must have a thousand of them. What does he need with another one?"

Hawk's expression was deadly serious. "He is going to be assassinated somewhere and sometime during his ten-day world tour."

"How do you know that?" I asked, relaxing only slightly.

Hawk handed a single sheet of paper across the desk to me, and while he talked I quickly scanned its contents, which appeared to be the transcript of a shortwave radio broadcast.

"The CIA intercepted that transmission three days ago from Lisbon. We don't know exactly where it was being directed, but we're assuming it was meant for someone in western Europe."

I looked up after a moment. "This is nothing more than some kind of a schedule, or maybe a very detailed itinerary."

"Right," Hawk said. "Now look at this one." He handed me a second sheet, this one labeled TOP SECRET and headed, PRESIDENTIAL ITINERARY.

It took me only a moment to realize that both pieces of paper contained exactly the same schedule. Whoever had sent the message from Lisbon had obviously known the president's travel plans down to the last detail, including hotel rooms and even the license numbers of the limousines that would be used to take the chief executive from place to place in each country.

"Those travel plans were given to the president's security service and the CIA only four days ago—one day before the Lisbon broadcast," Hawk said, chewing absentmindedly on his ever present cigar.

"There's a leak in the Secret Service, or more likely in the CIA," I said, handing the papers back. "So what? We've known that all along. As far as I've always been led to believe, it's one of the reasons AXE was created."

"Right," Hawk said tersely. "But why do you suppose someone in Lisbon would bother to send our president's travel plans to someone or some organization in Europe? And in fact, why would the Portugese be interested in such detailed plans in the first place? Two days ago the president announced his world tour to the press, listing the countries and cities he would visit, along with the dates. What reason would anyone have to want more detailed information?"

Hawk's message was coming over loud and clear. "Assassination," I said, half under my breath.

"Right again," Hawk said. "And we've been handed the job of stopping it."

"Why not the Secret Service itself?" I blurted, but then realized what I had just said.

3

Hawk started to protest, but I held up my hand. "I understand, sir," I said meekly. "Someone in Lisbon got the travel plans in the first place because there was a leak. Now if we tell the Secret Service that there will probably be an assassination attempt, the same leak will transfer the information back to Lisbon, who will in turn make damn sure their plans are foolproof."

Hawk nodded as he relit his cigar. "That's where you come in, Nick," he said, shaking out his match. "I want you to go along with the president on this trip. He'll be leaving Washington on the twenty-first, and you'll be with him as a personal bodyguard under his orders only."

"Does he know about the arrangement?" I asked.

"Yes, although he doesn't like it much. He's of the same opinion you are—he, too, thinks he has too many guards around him. But we've managed to convince him that this time it won't be just another Sirhan Sirhan or Lee Harvey Oswald taking a pot shot at him. If and when the try comes, it'll be more professional than that. And those two were successful."

I thought about that a moment. "If and when the attempt comes," Hawk had said. That meant a lot of sitting around with little or nothing to do until an attempt was made and I could get a handhold on this case.

"What about the Secret Service?" I asked. "What have they been told about me?"

"Absolutely nothing, Nick. And they are to know nothing. As far as they are concerned,

4

you're nothing more than another Secret Service man, but you've been handpicked by the president himself, and no one will give you any trouble. Under no circumstances can you blow your AXE identity.''

"What about my background?"

"Research has got that worked up for you," Hawk said. "You'll remain Nick Carter, but you've been with the CIA in their western-European division. You got sick of that business, asked for a transfer, and got stuck with the Secret Service. You don't like the assignment, but you've got it.''

This was just great, I thought. Not only was I going to have to hide from the assassins, whoever they were, but I was also going to have to hide under my cover identity from our own people.

Hawk was talking again, and I returned my attention to him.

"There's one thing about this case we haven't bcen able to figure, however," he said thoughtfully, as he examined the end of his cigar.

"Sir?"

"The Portugese. As far as we've been able to determine, both on and off the record, they have no reason to want our president dead. At least officially, he's well liked in Lisbon.''

"Maybe it's a splinter group, like the Arab terrorists," I suggested.

"No . . . '' Hawk hesitated a moment. "Portugese security is too tight for that, although the transmission may have been the work of some government faction we know nothing about.

That's part of your mission. I not only want you to thwart any attempt on the president's life, but I also want you to find out who is behind this and why."

Two days later I had cleared AXE headquarters and was given an immediate appointment to see the president. For now I continued to work out of my apartment, but I would soon be leaving with the presidential party. That gave me only a short time here in the States and then ten days overseas to figure out what was going on, and I figured I was going to be pretty busy, at least for a while.

"President Magnesen will see you now, Mr. Carter," the president's appointments secretary said to me as he came from the Oval office.

I quickly rose from the chair I had been sitting in for the last hour and followed the man into the president's office.

"Mr. Carter," the secretary announced, and then left, closing the door.

President Robert Magnesen was shorter and huskier than I had thought—not over six feet tall and 190 pounds or more. The times I had seen him on television, I had imagined him to be much taller and thinner. But his youthful, boyish face, longish hairdo for a man in his position, and fantastically charismatic smile came on even stronger in person as he got up and came around the large desk to where I stood. He held out his hand.

"David Hawk has told me a lot about you," he said in his Eastern accent. "And your service record is impressive."

6

I shook his hand and smiled uncertainly, wondering just what the hell Hawk had told him about me. "Thank you, sir," I said.

He indicated a chair for me, and he perched at the edge of his desk.

"As I told your boss, I'm not especially pleased to get AXE involved in something like this, and I'm not so sure that the Lisbon message is what it seemed to be. But for the moment I'm willing to go along with you."

"Yes, sir," I said. It was hard to look the man directly in the eyes. His gaze was penetrating, and it seemed that when he looked at you, no secrets could remain in your head.

But then he smiled again and chuckled. "Enough of a lecture. You're here assigned as a Secret Service personal bodyguard under my orders only. Derrick Stone—he's the head of the White House Secret Service contingent—is a good man. He'll probably fuss and fume a little because you're an unknown around here, but he'll get used to the idea. Besides, it will only be for ten days or perhaps less."

The last was said more in the form of a question to me, and I nodded. "I hope so, sir, but . . . "

"But what?"

"I don't quite know how to put this, sir," I started.

"Tell it straight, Carter. Like I said, the lecture is over. From this point on, I'm going to follow your orders as long as they don't get too silly. But if we're going to work together for the next week or so, I don't want any pussyfooting around. If you've got something to say, say it. I'll listen."

"Yes, sir," I said, somewhat relieved. At least I would not have to watch every little move I made for fear of offending some sensitive politician. And I had to admit I was beginning to like the president.

"All right then," he said, going back behind his desk and sitting in his chair. "What's in store for me?"

I sat forward. "First of all, Mr. President, we're fairly certain that there will be some assassination attempt. And like it or not, it has some Portugese backing. We're not sure if it's the government in Lisbon or just a faction group, but it does have support and therefore will be damned professional."

"How do you know that?" the president asked.

"Only a highly organized and well-financed group could have come up with your itinerary so fast," I said.

"We've had some pretty good relations with Portugal so far," the president said. "So whatever happens, I don't want any toes stepped on."

"That's not my job, Mr. President, it's yours," I said. "I'm here only to make sure that whenever and wherever the attempt is made, it's stopped. Additionally I am going to find out just who is behind this and if possible, why. What you will do with that information . . . " I let it trail off.

"I'm with you so far," the president said, a slight, wry smile playing across his handsome features. "How do you propose to do all that?"

"I'm going to be like your second skin. I'm hoping that the first attempt will be made fairly early in your tour, which will leave me time to run down that lead and see where it takes us.''

"First attempt?'' the president said, no longer smiling.

"Yes, sir. As I said before, this will be a professional job, and professionals do not give up with one or two failures. They'll keep trying either until you are dead or until I've run their organization down and wiped it out.''

The president thought about that for a moment. "Quite an assignment you've got yourself.''

"Yes, sir." I nodded. "Any one of hundreds of hotel employees, any one of ten thousand people lining a crowded street, any one of literally most of the world's population could be a triggerman waiting for just the right moment.''

"What do you want me to do?''

"Just act normal,'' I said. "But if I should knock you down or tell you to move, I'll expect you to instantly obey . . . sir. You can chew me out later if I was wrong.''

The president broke out into a loud laugh, and between gasps he managed to stammer, "All right, Carter, it's a deal.''

Meeting the president had been the easy part, I thought as I brought myself back to Kapiolani Park, where I stood a few yards to the side of the speaker's podium. About five thousand people had gathered so far, most of them sitting on the grass, picnic fashion, waiting for the president to arrive. This was going to be his kickoff speech for his ten-day world tour, and he wanted everything to

go perfectly. Television crews from all three networks had set up their mobile equipment, and the
podium bristled with a dozen or more micro-
phones.

Beyond the crowd, busy Honolulu was spread
out below us, and behind the podium the lush
foothills led sharply toward the base of the Koolau
Range, which was like a raised backbone for the
island of Oahu. To the left, rising up until it almost
blotted out that section of the sky, was the massive
Diamond Head, jutting out to sea.

An attack, if it happened here today, could come
from almost any direction. Anyone in the crowd
could be the assassin, and although Secret Service
men were stationed well back into the lush green
above and behind the podium, a professional could
make his way through the lines.

In the distance now I could faintly hear the
sirens from the presidential motorcade as it approached the park. But the sounds were a long way
off, and I knew it would be at least another five
minutes before they arrived.

Against my better judgment, the president had
convinced me that he would be perfectly safe riding from the hotel to the park in his bulletproof
limousine. He had suggested that I go ahead and
check out the area from which he would make his
speech. So far I had found nothing suspicious, but
it was like looking for a needle in a haystack. For
now I contented myself with standing by the
podium and waiting for the president's arrival.

After seeing the president on my first day of this

assignment, I had gone through the tough part, meeting Derrick Stone, who was as craggy and gruff a man as I have ever met.

Stone did not believe my cover story for one instant, but he was shrewd enough to realize that if the president had wanted him in on the real story, he would have told him everything. So although Stone did not like my presence on his security force, he was forced to put up with it.

His office was down the hall just a few steps from the president's, and when I was shown in, Stone greeted me with silence. After a moment I took out one of my specially blended cigarettes with NC embossed in gold on the filter tip, lit it, and sat down, matching the older man's steady gaze with one of my own.

Stone finally broke the silence. "I don't know what strings you pulled for this duty, or even why the CIA ever released you, but since you're here and evidently working directly for the president himself, there are a few things I am going to have to brief you on."

I nodded but said nothing. I had seen a lot of men like Stone over the past years. He was a professional, there was absolutely no doubt of that, but beyond his specific role he was like a fish out of water. Situations too far out of the ordinary—like the case I was assigned to now—would have been beyond his training. I had to admit though, that his job would be beyond me—and I would soon become bored with it. But Stone was not bored; in fact, he seemed to thoroughly enjoy what he was doing, almost to the point of being pompous. Although I've learned not to stick to first impressions or snap judgments, at this point I did not like Stone, and it was obvious the feeling was mutual.

"As you may already know," Stone continued, "the president is a very visible man. He does not like Secret Service personnel to get too close to him—it blows his image, I suppose. But it makes our job a damned tough one. How or why he decided to let you in and close to him is beyond me, but since you'll be closer than any of us, I'll expect you to do a good job."

I nodded and wondered idly what Stone would say and how he would react if he knew my true identity and what my mission was.

Stone handed across a single sheet of paper containing the president's itinerary—the same one that had been intercepted from the Lisbon broadcast and the same one that had been distributed routinely through channels to AXE.

I pretended to study it closely while trying to figure out just how the hell I could get out of his office without making him even more suspicious. I did not think I could stand too much more of his prattling.

But it wasn't to be. Stone kept me closeted in his office that afternoon for almost three hours, going over the president's likes and dislikes in infinite detail.

"Above all," he had said in parting. "The president does not like to be jostled. And if I see you are getting too damned close, I'll pull you off myself, no matter what he says about it."

"Yes, sir," I said, smiling and nodding.

My duties for the next three days consisted of

merely shadowing the president wherever he went, to get myself used to his routines. And then on the twentieth, yesterday, we had all boarded Air Force One for the flight west, stopping at Travis Air Force Base in California only long enough to refuel before we pressed on to Honolulu.

Now, ten hours later, the presidential motorcade was arriving at the park entrance and pulling up behind the podium, where the president emerged amid a crowd of newspeople and Secret Service men.

I could feel the blood begin to tingle and my heart begin to beat a little faster against my ribs as President Magnesen climbed the steps to the podium, waved at the cheering crowd, and then motioned for them to be silent.

The last strains of "Hail to the Chief" died out from the small brass band to one side of the speaker's platform, and Magnesen began to speak about the purpose of his world tour—which was, he said, to promote world peace through a new global economic cooperation that would lead to prosperity for all peoples.

As he spoke, I scanned the crowd, but nothing seemed out of the ordinary. Of course, it wouldn't, I told myself, as the president settled into his speech, which obviously was going to be a long one. You never knew when a hand would come up, a gun would be pointed, and several shots would ring out. No one had suspected it would happen in Dallas or in Los Angeles, but it had.

I strolled casually through the crowd pressed

nearest the podium, hoping against hope that if something was going to happen here today I would be able to catch a glimpse of a gun before it was too late. Very few people paid any attention to me as I moved about, and the few who did glanced my way only momentarily and then turned their attention back to the president, whose amplified voice boomed and reverberated through the park.

I was on my third circuit through the crowd, and Magnesen was just winding up his speech, when something caught my attention, and my hand went instinctively to Wilhelmina, my Luger, holstered beneath my sport coat. But then I stopped. What was it? What had caused the reaction?

And then I suddenly knew, as the dark shadow flashed once more over the crowd. I snapped around toward the podium and looked up in time to see a pale blue hang glider, almost invisible against the blue sky, floating gracefully in a large circle less than fifty yards from the president and less than a hundred feet off the ground.

I could make out the form of a man strapped in the harness, dressed in a pale blue jumpsuit, just as he raised what appeared to be an automatic weapon of some kind.

I ran several steps forward, pushing through the crowd to the open space between the front row of people and the podium, drawing Wilhelmina.

The hang glider was swooping down lower now and moving quite fast toward the president. I dropped to my knee as the president, suddenly becoming aware of my presence in front of him, stopped talking. I could hear the gasp rippling through the crowd.

I aimed my Luger with both hands, slightly leading the form dangling beneath the huge blue sail, and squeezed off a shot just as a spray of automatic fire slammed into the podium floor a few inches from the president. I quickly squeezed off another shot, and the assassin's head snapped back, the automatic rifle falling from his grasp. A third shot from my Luger hit him somewhere in the chest, and a spray of blood splashed down on the president, who had dropped to the floor beneath three Secret Service men. The hang glider swooped sharply to the left and crashed in the middle of the crowd, injuring at least a half dozen people, I was sure.

II

FROM THE MOMENT I had first spotted the hang glider until I quickly got to my feet could not have been more than twenty-five or thirty seconds, but already the president was being hustled into his waiting limousine by at least a half dozen Secret Service men, while others were converging on the would-be killer.

Most of the people in the large crowd had been stunned into inactivity by the shots, but now they were coming alive. Several women were screaming, some men were swearing loudly, and a mass exodus was already beginning.

Apparently the assassin had been working here alone, and there would be no further attempts, at least for the moment. But for a first attempt it had been very smooth.

I holstered Wilhelmina and pushed through the thinning crowd toward where the hang glider had crashed, about a hundred yards away. As I went, I scanned the area surrounding the park, stopping in midstride when my gaze came to Diamond Head. Of course. The hang glider had been launched from somewhere up the big peak. With the proper winds the man must have sailed for five miles or more, slowly and silently zeroing in on his target. Only the chance shadow from the giant kitelike wing had given him away.

If a cloud had been covering the sun, or if I had not chanced to look that way at just that moment, the president would now be dead, and the assassin would have floated gracefully off somewhere behind the park, no doubt to a waiting accomplice with a car.

But now, of course, the car would be long gone, surely untraceable and certainly unnoticed in all this confusion.

I reached the hang glider just as the distant sounds of ambulance sirens floated to us on the breeze.

Several people were lying on the ground around the huge metal-framed glider. At least two of them were probably dead. Several others were sitting holding their arms or legs, moaning. The assassin had been pulled from beneath the crumpled wreckage, and already Derrick Stone was checking through the pockets of his jumpsuit while one of his men was fingerprinting the dead man.

Stone looked up when I stopped just in front of him.

"Find anything?" I asked.

He scowled, then shook his head. "Not a thing except for this," he said, and handed up a loaded clip for an American-made AR15 automatic rifle. Then he straightened up and pulled me aside.

"Look, Carter," he said, his voice low, "I don't know exactly what's going on. But I do know that out of the clear blue sky you were assigned to be the president's handpicked personal man, and a few days later someone tries to assassinate him. I may be a big dummy, and maybe I'll never get any further than head of the presidential detail, but goddammit I can't work in the dark. What's going on?"

In his office Stone had been a dull, plodding bureaucrat, but out here in the field, and under fire, he had transformed into a highly efficient cop. My estimation of his abilities went up a couple of hundred percent.

"I can't tell you a thing, Stone. Not now. But as soon as we're done here, we'll have a little chat with the president. Maybe he can clear up a few things for you."

Stone searched my eyes for a long moment, then grunted. "Good enough for me, I suppose," he said, and then his lips curled into the faintest trace of a smile. "That was nice shooting."

I was about to nod my thanks, but he had already turned back to the assassin, giving orders to his people to have the body immediately removed to the city morgue.

The television-news crews had set up their equipment and zeroed in on the scene, but Stone had ordered them away, and now they were pulling their equipment back, as commentators faced the cameras, trying to explain what had happened.

I turned just in time to see one of the newsmen heading my way, and I hurried along with Stone and the others heading back to the president's hotel, but not before I had got a good look at the dead man's face, partially shattered from my second shot where I had hit him in the forehead over the right eye.

I rode in the back seat of Stone's car, crammed in with two other Secret Service men, as we raced out of the park toward downtown Honolulu. As we drove the dead man's features kept coming back into my mind's eye.

He had been a small man with dark, almost olive complexion. His hair was jet-black and well greased, and his fingernails were well manicured. His hands reminded me of the hands of a classical-guitar player.

That he was of Spanish origin I had no doubt. And I had even less doubt about his exact nationality.

It took only a few minutes to reach the president's hotel, but during that short time Stone was busy on the car's telephone giving orders at the morgue for an immediate autopsy, then contacting the local FBI to press them for a quick rundown on the assailant's fingerprints and mug shot from the vast but undiscriminating computer complex in

Washington, D.C. On my suggestion, Stone also called the CIA office in Honolulu and requested the same quick action from their Langley files.

"Within a few hours we should be getting something back," Stone said, turning to me after his last call.

"I doubt it," I half-mumbled.

He eyed me suspiciously but said nothing, and we pulled up in front of the Royal Hawaiian Hotel, piled out of the car, and marched into the lobby.

The president had the entire top floor of the twenty-seven-story luxury hotel all to himself and his aides. It had been reserved for him not as a luxury, but as a measure of security. Everywhere the president went he was always isolated from other people. It was the only way the Secret Service could have even a chance of keeping him alive. And that task seemed to be getting more difficult by the hour.

Only one elevator was in service to the top floor, and it, like the three sets of stairs up, was heavily guarded. Even though the three Secret Service men on duty at the elevator knew Stone personally, they still asked to see his ID card, as well as my own.

When we had passed inspection the elevator doors slid open and we were allowed to enter.

On the way up Stone said nothing more to me, but I could see that his mind was working like a set of high-speed gears. He was ready at any moment to explode in a flury of activity. I only hoped that the president would know the right buttons to push to calm him down.

The elevator came to a halt, and the doors slid

open, depositing us into the arms of three more Secret Service men. The ID routine was carried out once again, but Stone did not seem to mind. Now that the president was out of danger, at least for the moment, Stone seemed to have slipped back into his old mold of enjoying the heavy-handed bureaucracy.

This time both of us were frisked as well, and the quick examination turned up Stone's .38 Police Special, as well as my Luger, but not Hugo, my pencil-thin, razor-sharp stiletto in its chamois case just above my wrist, or Pierre, the tiny gas bomb AXE had developed for Killmasters, which fit into a specially designed pouch attached to my thigh, almost like a third testicle.

When we were finally cleared, we were shown down the corridor by one of the elevator guards to the presidential suite, where Stone knocked once and entered.

Inside, we were stopped in the foyer by the president's appointments secretary, who took our names and told us to wait until we were announced. Then he turned on his heel and went into the main room, leaving the door slightly ajar.

From inside I could hear what sounded like an argument, and I was able to pick out at least the president's voice among the voices of five men, one of whom sounded quite young.

Stone looked at me disapprovingly when he noticed that I was eavesdropping, but I merely shrugged. It was a natural instinct with me. The more information I had about any case I was working on, the happier I was. Eavesdropping, even on the president, was routine.

The loud, angry voices stopped a moment later, and then the appointments secretary—an older man with a neatly trimmed white moustache, dressed in an impeccable gray business suit—ushered Stone and me into the president's suite, and Magnesen rose to meet us.

He looked somewhat shaken by the experience, but he was recovering well. Five other people were in the room with him, and I recognized only two of them. One of them was the secretary of defense, who rose.

"Stone," the older man said, his voice booming surprisingly loud for a man of such slight stature, "maybe you can talk some sense into him. Apparently, we cannot."

"Take it easy, Bob—you're just overreacting," President Magnesen said to the man. Then he turned to us. "Come in and sit down, gentlemen."

Stone's manner had suddenly changed to nervousness in Magnesen's presence, and he perched on the edge of his chair, which had been pulled around to face the couch on which the president slumped. I sat in one of the easy chairs alongside Stone and surveyed the room, which seemed as big as a couple of football fields but was decorated with the peak of elegance and taste that could be found on the Hawaiian Islands.

Large sliding glass doors were open to let in the breeze because, as Stone had told me back in Washington, one of the things the president hated most of all was air conditioning. He had been an outdoorsman as a youth, and he disliked and mistrusted anything closed or confining.

Two security men were stationed on the balcony and would be relieved every four hours to make sure they did not become bored and therefore become lax in their vigil. They were equipped with high-powered rifles, hidden out of sight, and walkie-talkies. If trouble came from the outside, a pair of heavily armed helicopters would swoop down to cover the windows while Secret Service men from every floor in the hotel would converge on this suite.

For the moment, at least, the president was relatively safe. But how long we could keep him that way was a good question.

He was speaking to Stone.

"You people did a good job out there, Stone," he said in a soothing tone.

The secretary of defense and one of the other men grunted in disgust and turned their stares directly at Stone, who stiffened uncomfortably under their gaze.

"We were . . . uh . . . lucky, sir," Stone said almost timidly. "But we might not be . . . uh . . . the next time."

The president shifted his steady gaze to me, and I returned the stare.

"Stone is correct, Mr. President," I said carefully. "There is no real way to guarantee your safety if you continue with your tour." I was choosing my words and the tone of my voice very carefully. On the one hand, if the president did cancel his tour because of today's incident, I would be off the hook as far as this case was concerned.

But on the other hand, something inside me cannot stand to see a job left undone. And the only way this case was going to be solved was with bait, but the real item—the president himself.

The secretary of defense removed his glasses and shook his head. "There, you see, Mr. President, your own handpicked man, a man you told us was the cream of the crop from the CIA, a man you said you were assigning as your personal bodyguard, and a man who today saved your life with some fancy shooting—even he agrees with us."

The president smiled wearily, turning toward the defense secretary and the others—evidently cabinet members or advisors. "Gentlemen, I have every confidence in the abilities of Mr. Stone and his people, as well as Mr. Carter. But if someone wants badly enough to assassinate a president of the United States, they can do it just as easily in Washington as they can in Cairo or Peking or Paris or Bonn."

"Or Honolulu," the secretary of defense interjected. He turned around in his chair and called out across the room to a young man with extremely long hair, wearing faded dungarees, a sweat shirt, and dirty tennis shoes, whom I recognized as the president's somewhat radical son.

"Stanley, come over here and convince your father that he should cancel this trip."

Stanley Magnesen, who at twenty-five had been a student at Harvard for the last seven years, merely shrugged and glanced through the large sliding glass doors toward the beaches and the sea far below. His voice, when he spoke, was high pitched, almost a whine, as if he were chronically complaining about something.

"It won't do any good, MacDonald," the younger Magnesen said arrogantly. "Although I don't want Father to make this trip for a different reason than you, nothing I say or do around here is ever listened to anyway. I don't even know why the hell I ever agreed to come along in the first place."

The president was looking at his son with a slight amusement in his eyes, tinged with what seemed to me to be sadness.

Stanley turned after a moment. "One last time, Dad—don't make this stupid trip. You'll regret it." He took a step toward the center of the room, and he seemed suddenly to be warming to his subject. "Look, isn't it proof enough of what I've been telling you? Didn't you get the message today when that bastard came gunning for you? You were damned lucky to come out of it alive. But you should be grateful that you got the message before it was too late. No responsible, thinking, intelligent person on the face of this earth agrees with your plan for world peace through economic cooperation. No one. All you're talking about is spreading the American way to everyone else. Spreading the industrial-military complex around until every little country in the world is squeezed out of existence."

"That is enough," the president said quietly. Although I barely heard the words, Stanley evidently heard them quite clearly, because he bit off his next words and, after hesitating only a brief moment, wheeled and stalked out of the room.

The president turned back to us and chuckled. 'He's a headstrong boy. Once he gets out of this radical stage I'm sure he's going to be one hell of an international lawyer.''

No one else said anything. I guessed that this discussion had not been the first of its kind, even in front of the president's advisors. None of them seemed in the least bit stunned by the boy's outburst.

President Magnesen had turned back to me now. 'I wanted to thank you personally for saving my life, Carter. You did a splendid job.''

"That's why we came to see you, Mr. President,'' Stone spoke up.

The president eyed him carefully for a long moment, then turned back to his advisors. "If you don't mind, gentlemen, this is an internal-security matter. I'm sure you won't want to stay for the lurid details.''

The four men rose, but before they left, Secretary MacDonald stopped by the door. "There's nothing we can say or do to make you change your mind?''

The president shook his head. "This is too important, Bob. I can't cancel out now. The only thing that's going to save us from worldwide famine, and then war, is global cooperation to manage all food and mineral resources. I couldn't back out of this now even if I wanted to. Too much is riding on it. And I don't want to cancel out. No assassination attempt will stop me.''

Secretary MacDonald shook his head, and as he

went out the door with the others, I was sure I
heard him mutter something like "Stubborn ass,"
but the president ignored the comment, returning
his now businesslike attention to us.

"What have you two got for me?" he said
briskly.

Stone was the first to speak, and he sounded
extremely nervous. "Mr. President, it has come to
my mind that hiring Mr. Carter here from the CIA,
and the assassination attempt on you this afternoon, were just too coincidental."

The president glanced briefly my way but said
nothing, allowing Stone to continue.

"In order for me to work effectively . . . that is,
for me to do my job of protecting you with the
maximum efficiency, I must be made aware of any
and all facts concerning your safety and the mea-
sures taken to that end."

"What are you driving at, Stone?" the president
said, a sharpness still in his voice.

Stone seemed to be having some difficulties in
forming his next words, and his speech was halt-
ing. For a moment I almost felt sorry for the man.
After all, he was just trying to do his job the best
way he knew how.

"What I mean to say, sir, is if you are at all
dissatisfied with my work, with the way I am hand-
ling things, please say something and I'll resign. I
know I didn't do too well out there this afternoon . . ."

The president was laughing now, the humor
spread all across his face. For a moment Stone
looked as if someone had just cut into his insides.

with a sharp, hot knife.

"All right, Carter," the president said after a moment. "I guess we're going to have to tell him what's going on around here; otherwise, the best damned security man that ever guarded a president is going to quit on me."

I held my breath for a long moment. Hawk had said no one other than the president was to be made aware of my AXE identity or the role AXE was playing in this matter. But although Hawk was my boss, the president was his boss. So no matter how much Magnesen revealed now, I would be stuck with it. But my fears proved groundless, and my estimation of the president went even higher.

"Derrick, the story is simply this. If you suspected that Carter here was not exactly who he claimed he was, you were correct. He did not come from the CIA's western-European operation."

Stone's pained expression dramatically changed to one of almost triumph, and he sat forward in his chair. The president continued.

"He is CIA, however. From the Langley office. Clandestine Operations."

Although AXE considered the Clandestine Ops section of the CIA just as generally inept and bumbling as the rest of the vast organization, the majority of the world's population, including Stone, regarded the section as the top of the line in the intelligence community. To the world, Clandestine Ops included the James Bond super-sleuths—the heroes of the espionage world. No feat was too great for that section. And now Stone looked at me with new respect, and I guess I was wavering at that moment between pity for his naïveté and disgust for his sudden change in attitude.

But the president threw the ball my way now. "You tell him the rest, Carter."

For a moment I was at a loss for words. What the hell was I supposed to tell him? But then I realized what the president was trying to do. On one hand, Stone rightly needed to know enough about what was going on to do his job protecting the president. On the other hand, he couldn't be told too much, in case he was the leak or had contact with the leak that was siphoning information to the Lisbon organization. It was now my job to present Stone with a convincing story that he would believe and accept, one that would allow me to continue to work with relative freedom from suspicion.

"You heard the president's son a little while ago," I said, noticing a quick pained expression flash across the president's face. "Well, he was right on one point: What the president is trying to do with this world tour is not making him very popular with some factions. We got word through the Old Boy network a couple of weeks ago that there have been some rumblings of assassination attempts from almost every city the president will be visiting. So my chief thought perhaps you fellows could use an extra hand. Just to stay close to the president. A last line of defense."

Stone was nodding, but then his expression darkened slightly and he turned to the president. "But sir, why wasn't I told about this earlier?"

The president smiled. "Because, personally, until this afternoon I thought it was nothing more than a bunch of poppycock, and I didn't want to bother you with it. I only agreed to take on Carter here because the Clandestine Operations chief was making such a fuss."

Stone nodded again. "They were correct though, sir, if you'll pardon me saying so. If anyone in this business would know about something like this, they would. I'm glad at least that you let Carter come aboard. Look what happened this afternoon." He hesitated a moment, the difficulty in forming words coming back to him. "As much as I don't like to admit it, without Carter this afternoon, I'm not so sure my men could have stopped the assassination attempt. Carter did a fine job."

"Yes, he did," the president said immediately. "But don't underrate yourself, Stone. It was my fault for not making your information complete enough. You had to work under a handicap."

"Well, sir," Stone said, rising, "I think we can get back to work now."

The president rose with us. "What have you got on the assassin so far?"

"Nothing much, sir," Stone said. "But we're working on it. Should have something for you by this afternoon."

"And what about you, Carter?" the president said.

"That depends upon you, sir," I said.

"I'll be staying here in my room until I make my speech at the Punch Bowl early this evening."

"Good," I said. "That will leave me free this afternoon to check with my chief and see if he has any information on the assassin." I turned toward Stone. "Meanwhile Stone and I will check the arrangements for security tonight and tomorrow morning for your departure."

III

IT WAS NEARLY two-thirty by the time I was finally able to shake Derrick Stone and his inane prattling about how he had always wanted to get into Clandestine Ops but had never been able to pass the examinations. And despite my growing weariness with his sniveling attitude, I found myself in the position of praising his work as chief of the president's Secret Service detail. It was the only way I had found to stop him talking about me and my work with the CIA.

We were sitting across from one another at a table in the Honolulu FBI office, looking over mug books of known international terrorists—without much success, so far.

Nothing had come back from either the FBI files in Washington or the CIA files in Langley, and I was anxious to send off a coded twixt to AXE research to see if they had any information. But Stone had practically ordered me to remain and help with the mug books while his men were busy setting up the final security arrangements for the president's speech early this evening.

"Jesus Christ, man," I finally shouted in exasperation at him. "What the hell do you want? You've got the number-one security job in the nation. There's nothing higher. On your shoulders rests the responsibility for protecting the life of the most powerful man in the world."

"I suppose," Stone said, basking. "But I know I could have done a better job and would have been happier with the CIA."

I shook my head. "I don't think so. I think you're doing just fine where you are."

Stone looked at me sharply, now dropping all pretense of studying the open mug book in front of him on the table. "Just what the hell are you trying to imply, Carter?" he said peevishly.

And that did it as far as I was concerned. For once I didn't give a damn how suspicious he became, and I stood up abruptly.

"Take your beef to the president. I'm sure that when he finds out what you want to do, he'll arrange a transfer. Meanwhile, I've got too much work to do to sit around and listen to you cry in your beer about your missed opportunities."

I wheeled and started to walk away, but then stopped, not able to resist one last shot at the man.

"But let's just say for a moment that the president did pull some strings and get you assigned to Clandestine Ops. You wouldn't like it. It's not what you think it is. It's nothing more than a bunch of assholes sitting around trying to figure out what job to botch next. But then again, maybe you'd fit in quite well."

This time when I turned and started away I didn't stop, despite Stone's sputtered protests.

I don't often lose my temper, but every time I have, I've later regretted it. And already, stalking down the stairs and out the door to the bright Honolulu sunshine, I wished I hadn't lost it-this time. Nevertheless, I was still seething inside thinking about him. He was either the most colossal idiot who ever walked the face of the earth—in which case the president would not be safe even at a tea party with the ladies' auxilliary—or . . .

That thought stopped me cold as I was about to hail a taxi, and I stood at the curb with my arm raised. Or else Stone was putting on an act, pretending to be someone or something he was not.

But if that was the case, and he was not the bumbling idiot he made out to be, just what was he? Was he connected with the Lisbon organization, or was he suspicious of me and merely trying to throw me off-guard so that I would tip my hand and reveal who I really was? If so, he was a very shrewd man, and his tactics had already started to work on me.

From this point on, I cautioned myself, I would treat Derrick Stone as if he were the smartest intelligence agent the other side had ever come up with. It was the only way I could treat him and still have any confidence that my identity and mission would not be blown.

I stood motionless for a long moment before I realized that several passersby along the busy Honalaku Boulevard were staring at me. I dropped my arm as a taxi pulled up, and I got in.

"Amalgamated Press," I told the driver. He pulled out into the stream of early afternoon traffic.

It was three o'clock when I paid the cabby and entered the small, shabby offices of the Amalgamated Press Honolulu office. It had been at least five years since I had been here last, but it seemed that absolutely nothing had changed.

Since there had been little activity from this office for those years, Hawk had undoubtedly cut the budget, shifting a portion of its pitifully small working capital to the various trouble spots in the world where money always seemed to be a problem. It had been a wonder to me, ever since I had joined AXE, that although AXE did most of the real work, it had a tiny budget compared to the massive amounts available to the relatively useless and cumbersome CIA.

This station contained only two rooms in a medium-sized building that housed mostly real estate companies and one small pineapple wholesaler with a tiny warehouse in the rear.

The front room contained several desks, a half dozen clattering teletype machines, and a small counter for routine Amalgamated Press work. The windows were dirty, and the plastered walls were cracked and in bad need of paint. Near the rear of the room, however, an innocuous-looking door led to the bugproof safe room where the real business of this office was conducted.

When I entered, a young man came to the counter and smiled pleasantly at me. "Yes, sir?"

"Code gold," I muttered, half under my breath. These key words told any AXE employee in the worldwide that he or she was talking with a Killmaster or someone else very high in the limited AXE hierarchy.

The young man's face remained blank for a brief moment, and then it looked as if he would swallow his tongue when he realized what I had said.

"Yes, sir," he finally managed to stammer, as he regained his voice. "How may I help you?"

I nodded toward the safe room, and he almost turned and looked in that direction, but then his past training took over, and he suddenly became at least somewhat businesslike.

"If you would like to follow me, sir, we can discuss your newspaper contract in detail," he said loudly enough for the benefit of the other three young men in the room.

None of them looked up, however, as I came around the counter and followed the young man to the back room.

Once inside, with the door locked and the light switch turned on, its accompanying green light indicating that the electronic monitoring and scrambling devices were in operation, the young man once again seemed highly flustered. I made it easy for him. "No emergency, son," I said. "I'm

N3, and I want to send a twixt to Washington Research. Just routine.''

The boy's eyes nearly bulged out of their sockets with the mention of my Killmaster number, and as I sat down at the desk, he continued to stare at me from where he stood by the door.

Ignoring him, I opened the top desk drawer, pulled out a message flimsy form and quickly scribbled out the message I wanted to send. I merely gave a brief description of the man I had killed less than four hours ago. I pulled out a copy of his fingerprints, which I had managed to steal from the file Stone had started on the investigation, and included them with the message.

I was about to hand the flimsy up to the gape-mouthed boy, when another thought struck me, and I added a brief paragraph giving Stone's full name and description and asking for a brief rundown on his background.

At the end of the message I included the code sequence that meant I would stand by for the reply.

''I want this sent out immediately,'' I said, handing the message and fingerprint card to the boy. ''I'll stand by for the reply.''

''Yes, sir,'' the young man said, taking the forms from me.

The room we were in was small, not more than nine by twelve, and besides the desk and chair, it contained only one file cabinet and a small console that included a combination CRT teletype machine and facsimile unit for sending photographs or other visual items such as the fingerprint card.

I leaned back in my chair and lit one of my cigarettes inhaling deeply. The boy inserted the fingerprint card in the facsimile machine, lined up the light dot on the white border, and pushed the button that started the drum rolling. The dead gunman's fingerprints were on their way.

Sitting down at the CRT machine, the boy punched a sequence of buttons that not only connected this unit with a similar unit in our Washington office, but also started a completely automatic cryptographic machine that would encode any message sent.

It took only a few moments to send out the brief message, and when he was finished a green light winked on the console above the keyboard, indicating that receipt of the text had been acknowledged.

Then he swiveled toward me. "Mr. Carter?" he said hesitantly.

I smiled. "Yes?"

"Well, sir . . . ah . . . I just wanted to say that I've heard an awful lot about you. And . . . well, I just wanted to tell you that I admire your work."

I have never been able to take compliments very well, but for the moment this one threw me. How the hell did he know about me? Evidently my puzzlement showed on my face, because his lit up in a bright smile.

"I know a lot about you, sir. I worked in our Washington office up until last year as a cipher clerk. Used to see your stuff coming in all the time. I guess I sort of followed your career over the past five years."

"What are you doing out here?" I asked, for want of something better to say.

"I was promoted. This is my first real assignment."

"Station agent?" I asked.

"Yes, sir," he said nodding. "Nothing much has happened over this year, but it's good experience for me anyone, I suppose."

"Experience for what?" I asked, unable to help myself. This was almost a repeat of Derrick Stone.

"To be a Killmaster, sir. Just like you." The admiration was syrupy sweet in his eyes and his voice, making me groan inwardly. "I've been studying karate, been taking firing range lessons, and I've got a pretty fair command of three languages besides English."

"It's a good start," I managed to say with a straight face. There was no way I could tell this young man what I was really thinking. All the training in the world could not qualify him or anyone else to be a Killmaster. It takes a special kind of a personality, I guess, to do what we do. It's something we were born with. Some have called it brutality, which it is in a way, I suppose; others have labeled it ruthlessness, also true to a degree. Actually, it's nothing more than an abnormal development of the instinct of survival. Put me or any other Killmaster in a tight, life-or-death situation, and we'd be more likely to come out of it alive than almost any other person on the face of this earth, only because we just do not have the personality to give up, to resign ourselves to defeat. We must survive at all costs.

But how in the hell could I tell that to this kid? For that matter, why should I? If he had the instinct, which I doubted, he would push, shove, and claw his way to Killmaster status. If he didn't, he wouldn't make it and would never understand why, even if it was explained to him.

The boy fell silent after that, and I was satisfied to leave it there. But ten minutes later I was starting to get bored, just sitting here with him staring at me. I was about to suggest that he go out and get us some coffee, when the five-bell warning sounded from the CRT unit, indicating that a top-priority message was about to come in, and the boy swiveled around in his seat.

"Do you want a hard copy, sir?" he asked.

"No," I said, getting up from my chair and crossing the room to stand behind him so that I could look over his shoulder at the face of the picture tube. "I can read it from here."

"Very good, sir," he said. "It's coming in now."

The lines of the message printed themselves out across the face of the CRT.

The first few lines contained only the heading code. Below that, the body of the message was brief.

IDENT PRINTS MATCH DESCRIPTION FOLLOWS: SUBJECT'S ONLY KNOWN NAME: PORTENJO. PORTUGESE. KNOWN TERRORIST ACTIVITIES CONFINED LOCALLY 1973-75. RELEASED ESTORIL PENITENTIARY 6/15/76. NO KNOWN CRIMINAL ACTIVITIES SINCE.

DOB 11/27/44. NEXT OF KIN: UNK. AS-
SOCIATES: UNK. COMPUTER CROSS
INDEX CHECKING. FOR FURTHER INFO
QUERY CODE 7737 PORTENJO.

STONE, DERRICK T., CHIEF U.S. SECRET
SERVICE. ASSIGNMENT PRESIDENTIAL
DETAIL. ACCESS CLEARANCE. RATING
5A. AMENDED FIELD BACKGROUND IN-
CLUDES: DOB 3/15/31. GRAD UNIV MARY-
LAND 1/15/52. ENLISTED U.S. ARMY 1/16/52.
ASSIGNED INTELLIGENCE KOREAN
THEATER. DISTING. SERVICE CROSS,
ARMY COMMENDATION, KOREAN
MEDAL OF VALOR, CONG. MEDAL OF
HONOR. HON DISCHARGE RANK LT
COL. ASSIGNED SECRET SERVICE 6/1/60.
NUMEROUS PRESIDENTIAL CITATIONS
ON RECORD. FOR FULL REPORT QUERY
7738 STONE. E.O.M.

The last lines of the message shimmered, then
died on the screen before I was able to pull myself
away. It had not surprised me that where the CIA
and FBI had no information on the assassin, AXE
did, scanty as it was. But what really shocked me
was the information on Derrick Stone.

All along, I had naturally assumed that Stone
was a qualified man. Otherwise, he would not have
been assigned chief of the Secret Service detail
guarding the president. But never in my wildest
thoughts had I figured Stone to be a Medal of
Honor winner, with an army-intelligence background.

The man was obviously suspicious of me, was putting me in one hell of a fix. Not only did I have to do my assignment in secrecy, but now I had to play games with an honest-to-God hero, a man who was probably as shrewd as any I had ever come across judging from his record and performance so far.

I absentmindedly thanked the young man for his help and assured him there was nothing else he could do for me except forget that he had ever seen me. Then once again I found myself on the street hailing a taxi.

On the way back to the Royal Hawaiian Hotel I pondered my next moves. First I would have to tell the president not only what I had learned so far about this mysterious Portenjo with no first name, but then I would have to tell him about Stone, because at this point there was no way for me to put Stone off my trail effectively without arousing his suspicions even more.

The president was tied up in a conference when I got back to the hotel, and I was told that I would not be able to see him until after his speech tonight, unless it was an emergency.

His appointments secretary sniffed at me almost as if I had body odor, almost daring me to declare an emergency so that he could bother the president, telling him it was my fault that he had to be dragged out of an important meeting. But I did not rise to the obvious bait. I smiled instead and thanked the man to tell the president I would like to speak with him directly after his speech.

As I was leaving the top floor of the hotel, Derrick Stone was just coming out of his office, at the opposite end of the corridor from the president's suite. When he saw me at the open elevator doors, his features darkened into a scowl and he beckoned to me, his voice gruff.

"Carter, I want to talk to you. Now."

For a moment I toyed with the idea of ignoring him and continuing downstairs, where I intended to have a quick dinner before going out to the Punch Bowl to check on security arrangements. But something in Stone's manner told me that would not work this time. He was evidently still angry because of my comments earlier today, but there was something else in his commanding tone that started the warning bells jangling along my nerves.

The elevator doors closed as I turned and went back to Stone's office. Once inside, I sat down across the desk from him. As he had the first time we met in his office in Washington, he stared at me for a long moment before speaking.

"All right, Carter, now all bullshit aside. I want to know just what the hell is going on."

I gave him a blank look and shrugged my shoulders. "What do you mean?"

"When you left the FBI office this afternoon, I had you followed."

"I see." I nodded, my mind racing to find an alibi consistent with my cover story. Stone was becoming more than a nuisance, and on the off chance that he had turned sour and was the Lisbon contact, I had to consider him doubly dangerous.

"Well?"

"Well what?" I continued playing the game, my face a blank mask but my mind seething.

"You took a taxi directly across town to a building that contains the offices of a small wire service." He looked down at a sheet of paper in front of him on the desk. "Amalgamated Press." He looked up at me. "You were in there for twenty-seven minutes. Why?"

I looked around the room, as if searching for something or someone before I answered him, and his gaze instinctively followed mine.

"Outside of the States, Clandestine Ops sometimes uses Amalgamated Press or some other wire service for message drops. We usually send the coded message to Langley through the New York office."

"And?"

"And, I wanted to use the Old Boy network again this afternoon to see if we had anything on the assassin."

"And?" Stone said relentlessly. He obviously was not believing a thing I was telling him. But I could not reveal the information I had on the man called Portenjo, because if Stone was the Lisbon man, my knowing the assassin's identity would tip the organization off, making my job next to impossible.

"And nothing. We didn't have a thing on him."

There was a satisfied smirk on Stone's face. "We checked out the Amalgamated Press after you left. The office manager, under pressure, told us essentially the same thing." His suspicious manner relaxed somewhat, and I made a mental note to send a letter of commendation for the young man at the Amalgamated office.

"Why did you follow me?" I said, a tinge of suspicion in my own voice. It was the only way to throw him off the track.

"Because I didn't trust you," he said matter-of-factly.

"And now you do?"

He looked at me for a long moment and then finally nodded. "Yes, I do. But I don't like you. The sooner this job is done, the better I'll feel."

I rose to leave, but he stopped me. "Where are you going now?" he asked sharply.

"For some dinner, and then I'm going out to the Punch Bowl."

"All right," he said after another moment. "Keep your eyes open. I'll see you there."

IV

THE PRESIDENT'S SPEECH at Honolulu's famed Punch Bowl open-air auditorium went without incident, although the place was packed with an estimated twenty thousand people. By midnight the presidential party, myself included, had loaded aboard Air Force One and were on our way to Tokyo, where the president would spend two days talking with the Japanese prime minister, visiting a few of the Tokyo sights, and making a speech at the imperial palace.

During the long trip I slept only in brief snatches, thinking about what I had learned, and what I had not learned, so far.

The first and foremost item was that Hawk's theory had been correct: The Lisbon message did spell assassination. I was only half-surprised that another attempt had not been made at the Punch Bowl. One explanation that kept popping into my mind was that the assassins, too, had their own itinerary. At this moment, I figured, they were probably setting up for their second attempt for Tokyo. It was going to be a busy couple of days.

The second item was Derrick Stone. There was no doubt in my mind that the man was still suspicious. If he had been a less qualified man, his suspicion would not have bothered me so much. But now I knew that his sniveling attitude in the FBI office in Honolulu had been nothing more than an act carefully conceived to make me lose my temper and do or say something that would reveal my true identity. I only hoped that his inquiries at Amalgamated Press had been passed on to Washington, where Hawk would have been alerted. My cover would withstand plenty of scrutiny from the outside, but if I were to operate effectively on this mission, my cover would not hold up well from the inside. Stone would continue to be a thorn in my side until he was somehow sidetracked. And that, I told myself for the tenth time, had to be my number-one priority.

Two more items kept my mind busy during the flight. The first was the president himself. He had been too busy to talk to me before his speech, and he had claimed he was too tired afterward. He had been hustled aboard the waiting Air Force One directly after his speech, and he had retired to his private cabin before takeoff. Since then I had not seen him.

The one impression I had got, however, from seeing him during his speech and then catching glimpses of him as he was taken out to the airport, was that somehow he was a changed man. It looked almost as if he had learned something that was worrying him intensely. It was not like Magnesen, and I was determined to find out whether his concern had anything to do with me or my mission.

It was unlikely that Stone could have said anything to him to make him suspicious of me. But something had got to him, and if it was going to affect my mission capabilities, I wanted to know about it.

That was the last thing to occupy my mind before I fell asleep.

The change in the pitch of the jet engines woke me up, and I sat forward with a start. The lights in the main cabin of the jet were on dim, but toward the rear of the aircraft, where the conference table was, the main overhead lights were on.

It was nearly six o'clock, and I looked out the window at the ocean far below. In the distance I could dimly make out a coastline, which I assumed as Honshu, the main Japanese island. The sun was just coming up, but even at this distance I could see a mass of clouds over the island. It was probably raining right now in Tokyo, which could make an assassin's job somewhat easier. It would be harder to spot an outside attempt with the visibility hampered by rain.

I got up from my seat, and Derrick Stone, who was seated at the conference table with four other Secret Service men, beckoned to me. I headed back to them as I took out a cigarette, lit it, and inhaled deeply.

Air Force One, an aging Boeing 707, was scheduled to be replaced next year with a 747. But despite the age of this aircraft, it was still luxurious. The president had his own bedroom and bathroom at the rear of the airplane, isolated from the remainder of the aircraft by a wall. In his cabin he had a communications console that would put him in touch with all the armed forces of the United States and its allies, as well as a hotline to the Kremlin. Sitting outside the president's door, day and night, was an army warrant officer with a briefcase padlocked to his wrist. The briefcase contained the ever present war codes, another symbol of the president's awesome power and responsibility. Although I've been in tough spots, I don't think I could ever handle the pressures of his job.

"We're going over the president's itinerary for Tokyo," Stone said, looking up, as I pulled out a chair and sat down across the table from him.

The others nodded to me, and I returned the greeting, then turned my attention to Stone. "I assume your advance men have already started the setup for us," I said.

"Right," Stone said, "but I've got something else for you."

I sat forward in my seat. I didn't like his tone of

voice—he sounded almost smug. But I said nothing, waiting for him to continue.

"You've met the president's son, Stanley," Stone began, and I nodded. Some of the other men smiled slightly.

"Well, Stanley's girlfriend will be joining the presidential party in Tokyo later this morning, and she plans to continue on the remainder of the trip."

"So what?" I asked, a little too sharply. Stone continued as if I had not said a thing.

"The president has asked that you be assigned not only to him, but to his son and his girlfriend as well."

"What?" I rose half out of my seat.

Stone was smiling. "You can talk with the man later this morning if you'd like. But that's the word he gave me last night."

"Why wasn't I included in that briefing?" I asked.

Stone shrugged. "I have no idea, Carter. The president just pulled me aside last night on the way to the airport and gave me the change in orders."

Something was wrong here. Combined with the president's strange, distant behavior toward me yesterday afternoon and evening, this change in assignment was doubly strange. Having to play baby-sitter for Magnesen's recalcitrant son and the boy's girlfriend would effectively hamper my work. If the order had really come from Magnesen, there had to be some reason behind it. But whatever it was, it would have to wait until I could get him alone. If I was going to have to remain with

Stanley and the girl, I would request a transfer off this assignment. If I was going to do a job, I wanted to do it right or not at all.

Stone was still talking. "The girl is Olanda Williamson. She's twenty-six, a writer for the *Saturday Review* and a couple other intellectual magazines."

"And I suppose I'm supposed to baby-sit her and the president's son?"

"That's right," Stone said, but then his attitude softened. "It's really not that bad, Carter. The president has top priority, so the only time you're going to have to be with the kids is when they are with the president or when the president is in his hotel room or with the prime minister at government center."

As far as I could figure it now, I had only two options. If I was going to have to play baby-sitter, I'd be constantly busy, never having any time to work on my own. So I was going to have to explain the situation either to the president or Hawk. And I had a funny feeling that now, for some reason, it would do no good to talk to Magnesen.

"What's the schedule for this morning?" I asked.

Stone referred to his sheet for a moment, then looked up. "You're on your own, actually, until around noon. There will be a small reception for the president when we land in twenty minutes. Then he, Stanley, and the others will be going to the Imperial Palace, where they will stay until after lunch. Miss Williamson will be meeting them there."

"And after that?" I asked, thankful at least that I was going to have this morning off.

"You're not going to like this next part," Stone said. "None of us do."

"Go ahead," I said resigned, to almost any kind of insanity.

"The president, Stanley, and Miss Williamson, as well as the rest of the presidential party, will be taking a walking tour of the Ginza. That's Tokyo's entertainment and shopping district."

"I know it," I said. "But you've got to be kidding. Security will be impossible."

"I know, I know," Stone said, nodding. "But tell it to the man. He insisted."

"Christ! What comes after that?"

"A speech at three outside the Imperial Palace and then a parade at four-thirty."

"And tomorrow?"

"The president will be closeted with the prime minister at government center most of the day. His son and Miss Williamson however, will be taking the grand tour of the city. So you'll have to baby-sit them until after the reception and dinner at the Imperial Palace that night. The next day we leave for Peking."

It was well after seven o'clock, Tokyo time, by the time Air Force One had landed, the president had been met by a small brass band that played "The Star Spangled Banner" and "Hail to the Chief," and the president had been whisked away to the Imperial Palace.

I was to follow with the security-service contingent, but I begged off, telling them I was going to do some snooping around the Ginza and then along the parade route.

"Stay the hell out of trouble," Stone cautioned me. "And make damned sure you're back at the Imperial Palace at noon."

After assuring him I wouldn't dream of missing the walking tour, I took one of the small Toyotas at our disposal and hurried into the center of Tokyo, the sprawling metropolis of nine million people, the second largest city in the world.

Five years ago I had been here on another mission that had nearly cost me my life. That mission had begun with the death of my best friend, whose fiancée was the girl I wanted to see this morning.

Kazuka Akiyama had fallen for me near the end of that mission, probably for the same reasons she had fallen for my best friend. In many respects the two of us had been very much alike.

But now five years had passed without any word from her, and I wondered if she still remembered me and if she still felt the way she had. When I had left Tokyo that time, she had made me promise to come back to see her.

Now I was finally here.

I did not go directly to her apartment, the address of which I had gotten from the AXE directory in Washington. I took a roundabout route that brought me more than once through the Ginza district. If Stone or his people were following me, I wanted to lose them, but first I wanted to convince them that I was doing exactly what I had told Stone I would be doing—checking out the route the president would be taking later today.

Also, I did not think a visit to an apartment in Tokyo and a later visit to another Amalgamated Press office would do much for my already shaky standing with Stone. The less suspicious Stone was about me, the easier my job would be.

After an hour of driving, however, I was satisfied that if there had been a tail behind me, I had lost him. I parked on a side street about a block from Kazuka's apartment, going the rest of the way on foot.

The building she lived in was only three stories tall, the entrance hidden by a privacy screen along the front, with many flowering plants.

Kazuka's name was listed for 1A, on the ground floor, and I buzzed her apartment. It was after eight, and now as station manager for Amalgamated Press here in Tokyo, there was a good chance she would already be at work. But a moment later she was on the intercom.

"Yes?" her voice sounded tiny over the speaker.

"Kazuka? This is Nick Carter. May I come in?"

There was a long silence, but then the buzzer for the inner door sounded, and I went into the corridor.

I had just gotten through the door and started down the hallway, when Kazuka's door opened and she stepped out to watch me come down the hall. She wore only a thin kimono and her hair was up in a towel. Evidently she had just gotten out of the bath.

If anything, she was more beautiful than I remembered. The years had been more than kind to her. She stood just a little over five feet, with a small button nose, soft oriental eyes and complexion, and the most pleasing smile I have ever seen on a woman.

"So it is you," she said softly in Japanese, a language I can understand well but can't speak very pleasingly.

For an awkward moment we stood looking at each other, and then she was in my arms, and I could feel her shudder and then sigh. When we parted there was a tear on her cheek. I kissed it away.

"That's better," I said gently, and led her back into her apartment. Delicately arranged flowers adorned the few simple cabinets and hutches around the master room, which in Western countries would serve as a living room. Subtly done watercolors were hung on the walls, complementing the beautifully decorated *tatami* mats on the floor.

I had left my shoes by the door, and now Kazuka helped me off with my coat and tie. But instead of offering me the customary house jacket, she continued undressing me.

Soon we were nude, and she was in my arms again as we slowly sunk to the soft mats on the floor.

"Nick . . . oh, Nick, it has been so long!" she cried. "I did not think you would return."

I said nothing, and soon we were making love. Gently. Slowly. With no hurry or apparent concern for anything else in the world. Besides watercolors and floral arranging, the Japanese are also very expert at lovemaking. Kazuka was no exception.

Her body, lithe and strong from her AXE training, was perfectly adapted for this fine art, and I lost myself completely under her ministrations.

Her small, firm breasts, the nipples still erect, brushed against my chest when we were finished, and she looked down at me with obvious love in her eyes.

"I have waited for a very long time for this, Nick Carter," she said, switching to English.

Five years ago we had wanted each other, but then it had been too soon after the death of her fiancée, my best friend, who had been AXE's Tokyo station manager. But now, Kazuka had been everything I had imagined she would be.

I smiled up at her. She was lying on her side, propped up on one elbow, studying my face.

"You are beautiful, little Kazuka," I said in Japanese.

She laughed. "English, please," she said.

I laughed with her. "Like the lotus flower, my little one, you are pleasing not only to my eyes, but to my touch and my nose." I said it in the formalized Japanese.

A sad smile played across her features, and she sat up, reached over to the low table nearby, and lit us a cigarette. When she turned back to me and placed the cigarette between my lips, she studied my face.

"You are on an assignment?" she asked softly.

I took a deep drag and exhaled the smoke slowly as I nodded.

"And you are here for help or information from me?" she continued.

Again I nodded. "I'm sorry, Kazuka. I wish it could have been another way."

She sat up again and shook her head. "Do not be sorry, my love. It is our job. I am only happy that we were able to spend at least this small time together. I have dreamed often about you . . . about this moment."

"As I have," I said, touching her bare shoulder.

She shrugged away from me, stood up, and gathered her kimono, which she put on and belted tightly. I remained where I was, on my back on the *tatami,* smoking the rest of the cigarette while she fixed us a drink. When she came back and sat down beside me her attitude had changed from sadness to professionalism.

"What is it you need, Nick?" she asked in English.

"The president is here in Tokyo, as you know," I began. She nodded but said nothing.

"There was an attempted assassination in Honolulu yesterday."

"I know. It was on all the news," she said. "Do you expect another attempt here in Tokyo?"

I nodded. "We picked up a radio transmission from Lisbon a couple of weeks ago. It gave the president's itinerary for this trip. They failed in Honolulu, so I'm certain they'll try again here."

"I've heard nothing, Nick—" she began, but I cut her off.

"I did not expect you would, but I'll need some help from you. The president and your prime minister are going on a walking tour through the Ginza this afternoon.''

She groaned.

''I'll need some of your people, low profile, to hang around his route. Just keep a lookout for anything or anyone who might look interesting.''

''There's no way you can guarantee his safety in Ginza,'' she said thoughtfully. ''Make him cancel.''

I shook my head. ''I can't. But with your people in place it'll make our job a little easier.''

She thought about that a moment. ''How about later?''

''There'll be a parade this afternoon, and after that he'll be at the government center, in conference tonight and tomorrow. If anything is going to happen, it will be this afternoon. Either in the Ginza, which is the most likely, or possibly along the parade route.''

Again Kazuka seemed lost in thought, and when she came out of it, she looked at me, the same sad expression on her face, then reached down and ran her fingertips across my chest.

''You are a lovely man, Nick Carter. But one not for me.''

I started to protest, but she put her fingers on my lips. ''Not now, my love,'' she said gently. She put down her drink, took mine and set it aside, and then took off her kimono again and began carressing me with her entire body in a way only the Japanese can.

It was quarter to five and every nerve in my

body was tense with expectation as the president left the podium outside the Imperial Palace and got into his limousine.

Absolutely nothing had happened in Ginza. The president's walking tour had gone completely without a hitch. I had walked along a few feet behind and to one side of the president, where I spotted at least a few of Kazuka's people, but no suspicious person. The crowds had been thick, especially with women and children. By the time the president climbed into his limousine with the Japanese prime minister to head for the Imperial Palace, I was drenched in sweat and Stone seemed on the verge of collapse.

"One down, two to go," Stone said to me as we followed the presidential limousine in the small Toyota.

"The speech and the parade?" I had offered.

Stone, who was driving, had nodded. "After that it'll all be gravy. He'll be mostly closeted with the PM in the government center. It'll be a snap."

Several thousand people had gathered outside the gates of the Imperial Palace to listen to the president's brief speech, which had just concluded, and many thousands more lined the parade route, which led from the palace for three miles along the Hibiya-Dori Avenue of modern department stores, boutiques, and other highly Westernized businesses.

All that was left now was the parade. If there was going to be an attempt on his life, it would come here, within the next forty-five or fifty minutes.

The president's limousine traveled the parade route directly behind a Japanese honor guard of fifty motorcycle cops, each cycle festooned with an American flag as well as the Japanese white flag with orange sun.

The entire procession, including the floats, dragons, and bands behind the limousine, moved down the crowded avenue around three or four miles per hour, so Stone and, I along with a dozen other Secret Service men, walked along, surveying the crowd as we went.

Four Secret Service men were sitting on the four fenders of the large black Cadillac, their right hands inside their coat pockets, their fingers no doubt gripping the butts of their guns.

I had been tense in Ginza and even more worried during the president's speech, but now, halfway through the parade route, the hairs on the nape of my neck were standing up, and my stomach was doing its flipflops, as it always does when my intuition tells me something is about to happen.

When it did happen, I almost missed it. Stone, walking behind the limousine on the opposite side from me, said something, and I started to turn toward him, when a motion caught my attention out of the corner of my eye.

I turned fully around in time to see a young man, dressed in a very long and bulky overcoat, burst from the crowd and race toward the president's limousine.

Instantly my legs were moving and in a few steps I had intercepted the young man and tackled him. We both went down in a heap on the street.

I looked up in time to see a boot coming my way and managed to turn my head far enough to one side so that the blow only glanced off my cheek. But it was enough so that the young man broke away from my grasp, jumped up, and leaped toward the limousine as he reached inside his coat. I shouted something at the men on the limousine, who had still not realized anything was going on.

It seemed to take forever for the Secret Service man who had been sitting on the back right fender to turn around, see what was happening, and jump off toward the young man.

Then it all happened in double time. The large Secret Service man, Stan Larsen, literally jumped atop the young Japanese. They both went down, twenty feet from me, and as I was getting to my feet an explosion sent Larsen three feet into the air, blood and bits of human body tissue flying everywhere.

There would be no help for Larsen or for the Japanese terrorist, but there were others.

The president's driver, finally realizing what was happening, had sped up and was pulling around the motorcycle contingent, when another young man, also dressed in a bulky overcoat, emerged from the crowd, nearly half a block from me.

I pulled out Wilhelmina, dropped to my knee, and with both hands on the gun, squeezed off a shot. The shot missed as the limousine came closer to the young man, who started to reach inside his coat.

If he got to the trigger of the bomb and set it off

when the president's limousine was next to him, the Lisbon organization would be successful.

Holding my breath and taking what seemed like an eternity to make sure of my shot, I squeezed off another round. The young man's hands flew up, away from his coat, and he fell backward as the limousine with the president and the Japanese prime minister raced by.

V

"PLASTIQUE," STONE SAID, looking down at the young Japanese man I had shot and killed.

His overcoat had been pulled back to expose row upon row of tubular packages sewn to the lining of the coat and wired together to a detonator switch. My bullet had slammed into the man's chest about a half inch from the firing device.

Stone stared at me for a long moment, oblivious of the police efforts to clear the street and of the pressing, jostling crowd of newspeople. "Seventy yards with a handgun," he said.

I shrugged. "I missed the first shot."

Stone looked back down at the dead man. "And

damned near blew this kid and the president sky high."

"Wasn't any time for anything else—" I started to say, but Stone waved me off.

"I didn't meant it that way, Carter," he said. He looked weary, about ready to collapse. "Once again I find myself in the position of thanking you for doing my job."

I didn't answer; instead, I looked up at the growing crowd of newspeople as a flashbulb went off, and Kazuka Akiyama lowered her camera. I turned back to Stone.

"We'll have to try for an ID on this man as well. Maybe Washington will have something on him," I said loudly enough so that Kazuka could hear me. From the corner of my eye I could see her moving away from us and heading back, presumably to the first body to take another picture. I was sure that within the hour, the photos would be developed and on their way by facsimile to Washington research. Sometime this afternoon or evening AXE would have come up with something. Kazuka was one hell of an efficient woman, out of bed as well as in.

Stone was about to reply, when the ambulances finally arrived. We turned and watched as the bodies of the Japanese man and Stan Larsen were loaded aboard. Kazuka made it to them just in time to get a picutre of the Japanese before his face was covered with the sheet.

"He was a good man," Stone said when the ambulances pulled away.

I nodded.

"He's got a wife and three kids back in Arlington. I hope they understand what he did."

It's not that I'm particularly crass or hard or emotionless; it's just that I've always had the firm conviction that life is for the living. "I'm going to talk to the president," I said.

Stone looked at me. "Good idea. I think we should load him aboard Air Force One tonight and hustle him back to Washington. We do have that power, no matter what he says."

I turned without another word, comandeered one of the Secret Service Toyotas, and hurried across town to where the preisdent had been taken to his suite in the Imperial Hilton.

In twenty minutes I had arrived, had been checked through security, and was being led to the shaken president by his completely subdued and now very respectful appointments secretary.

The president was seated, drink in hand, on the couch across from where his son, Stanley, was seated in a comfortable-looking easy chair. No one else was in the room, and it looked as if the two had been arguing again—violently. Stanley's face showed the signs of strain, but when I entered the room he managed a slight smile.

"Thank you, Mr. Carter," he said rising and holding out his hand to me. "Thank you very much for saving my father's life for the second time."

I took the young man's hand, and his grip was surprisingly firm.

"I'm sure you and my father had much to discuss, so I will leave you now. But I'd like to talk with you when you're finished here."

For an instant I wondered what Stanley could possibily want to talk to me about, but then I dismissed speculation and nodded. "Sure thing," I said.

Stanley nodded to his father and then turned and went out of the room.

When he was gone the president looked up at me. "Fix yourself a drink, Carter."

I shook my head and perched on the edge of the easy chair that Stanley had just vacated. "Never drink when I'm trying to think, Mr. President."

The president raised his glass to me in a salute and took a deep drink. "Once again I have AXE to thank for my life."

"Are you going to cancel the rest of your trip?" I asked without mincing words.

The president hesitated a moment. "In Honolulu my answer was absolutely not. I am committed. But now . . . " he let it trail off for a moment. "But now I'm not so sure. Maybe Stanley is right. Maybe MacDonald is right. Maybe what I'm trying to do is so universally unpopular that they'll keep on trying until they get me, unless I give this up."

I shook my head. "That's not true, Mr. President, and I think you know it. The Lisbon message indicated that this is one group after you. A number of fanatics—professionals, nevertheless—want you dead for some reason. It may or may not have something to do with your world-peace plan, but that is really irrelevant. I don't think your plan is universally unpopular. You personally are unpopular with this one group of terrorists. That's all."

The president drained the last of his drink, set the glass down on the coffee table, sighed, and then straightened his shoulders. "You're correct, of course, Carter. So what's the next step?"

Was I right? For a moment my conviction wavered. If I was right, then at best the president would be in extreme danger for the next few days. But if I was wrong, then his decision would surely be fatal. He was a good man. I had come to respect him more than any other man I have ever known, except perhaps for Hawk, who sometimes, in a weak moment, I thought of almost as a father.

"Your decision, Mr. President," I said. "If you cancel your trip and return to Washington, my job of tracking these people down will probably be impossible. Then you won't be in any danger. But in effect they will have won anyway. They will have stopped you. On the other hand, if you continue on this trip you'll not only be placing yourself in extreme danger, but you'll have to fight your son, by the looks of it, as well as Stone, who will probably exercise his Secret Service option of ordering you back to Washington."

"I can get around Stone," the president said thoughtfully. "He will listen to me."

I nodded.

"And I'm not particularly worried about the danger. I am worried about what effect these attempts are going to have on my talks—especially in Peking and Moscow. It might make them jumpy."

"Your territory again, Mr. President," I said. "But if you decide to continue, I'll ask you to take a number of precautions."

The president looked at me for a long moment, and finally he nodded. "I'm continuing. I can take care of Stone and MacDonald, and as far as Stanley goes . . . well . . . "

"First," I said, getting up from the chiar, "I want you fully armed. I assume, sir, that you can use a handgun."

The president smiled. "I was top man in my company in the army. As the C.O. I was a better marksman than the kids."

"Second," I continued, "from this moment on, whenever you step out of this room, I want you wearing a bulletproof vest. One of the Vietnam flak jackets. They're hot and uncomfortable, but it could save your life."

"Agreed," the president said.

"And finally, you go nowhere or do nothing without my express approval. If I'm tied up and you can't get the message to me, sit tight."

That rankled with Magnesen; I could see it in the slight stiffness in his features. But he finally nodded. "Agreed," he said tightly.

"I want to bust this organization, Mr. President," I said. "But I also want to keep you alive. I think you are one hell of a president. I don't want my country to lose you."

The president rose and shook my hand. "All right, Carter," he said, smiling for almost the first time this afternoon. "You win. I'll be a good boy."

"How about this evening?" I asked him.

"I've canceled the reception. I'll remain here."

I nodded. "And tomorrow?"

"Government center."

"You'll be safe there," I said. "And after that you'll be in Peking. I'm sure that you won't be in any danger in China or in the Soviet Union. Their state police are too efficient for that. Besides, a president of the United States being assassinated on Chinese soil would start World War III. The Chinese simply will not allow it."

"A sad commentary on our system," the president said, and I agreed.

It was just a little after seven-thirty when I left the president. Stone was talking with Stanley in the corridor, and when I came out they both looked up.

"What'd he say?" Stone asked me.

"He's going to continue—" I started, but that's as far as I got before Stone and Stanley both burst out in angry shouts.

Stone overrode the younger man. "I'm going to exercise the Secret Service act. I'm taking him back to Washington."

"I think he wants to talk with you first," I said.

Stone was about to protest further, but then he sighed. "He wants to see me now?"

I nodded, and Stanley broke in. "Mr. Carter?"

I turned to him.

"Will you be on the detail coming along with Miss Williamson and me this evening?"

I was about to say no, but something in Stanley's eyes changed my mind. I don't know what it was—it seemed as if he was almost pleading with me but could say no more in front of Stone. I finally nodded. "When do we leave?"

"Good," Stanley said, smiling. He looked at his

watch. "We're to pick up Miss Williamson in her room downstairs in five minutes."

"Fine," Stone said to Stanley, and then he patted me on the arm. "When you return to the hotel this evening, I'll have something for you. I think we'll be moving the man out first thing in the morning. Early. We'll go over the details."

"Okay," I said, and Stone entered the president's suite as I went down in the elevator with Stanley to meet his girlfriend.

For more than two hours we traipsed around Tokyo—Stanley Magnesen, his girlfriend Olanda Williamson, myself, and five other Secret Service men, as well as a cadre of at least twenty newspaper and television reporters.

We had drinks at three clubs in the Ginza, made brief appearances at two nightclubs downtown, took a quick tour of the harbor area lit up at night, and finally, at ten o'clock, we ended up atop the Tokyo Television tower, which rose one thousand feet into the night sky, all the city spread out below us.

I had come along on this jaunt under the impression that Stanley had wanted to talk with me, but if he did, he hid it well. More than once when we could have talked, at least briefly, Stanley avoided any discussion. Now I was tired, not only physically, but of a spoiled little boy's antics.

Olanda Williamson, on the other hand was charming—almost too charming. Standing at least five feet ten, she had the luxurious platinum-blonde hair, with the makeup and clothing to go with it, that you might find adorning a New York model, not a writer for a number of intellectual magazines.

She could and did converse knowledgably on a wide range of subjects, and throughout the night she seemed to make sure that I caught ample glimpses of her lovely thighs through the side slit in her dress as well as plenty of cleavage whenever she bent down—which seemed often.

Stanley was playing a game—cops and robbers, probably—with me, and so apparently was Olanda; but her game was of a totally different nature.

I had been expecting something to happen with Olanda all through the night, so it came as no surprise to me when, as Stanley was cornered by reporters in the souviner shop near the top of the tower, Olanda slipped away.

Stanley agreed to the impromptu press conference, and I was able to slip away as well, to follow Olanda. She had taken the set of stairs that led another thirty feet up to the small observation room just below where the television antennas were.

The tower had been closed off to the public during this tour, so when I got upstairs Olanda and I were alone. She apparently had been expecting me, because she did not turn around; instead, she continued to stare out at the city below.

"It's lovely up here, isn't it, Nick?" she said softly.

I came up behind her and stood looking over her shoulder at the city. "Let's go back to the others before Stanley gets himself into trouble.''

"Let's not," she said softly, and she suddenly turned to face me, threw her arms around my neck, and kissed me passionately, her tongue darting around my lips as she rotated her pelvis against mine.

I tried to push her away, but she clung more tightly to me, kissing my neck and ears. "God, Nick, please! I need you!" she said huskily. "We've got time. No one will come up here."

She pulled back from me and started to hike up her dress. I reached out and slapped her hard across her face, and for a moment she was stunned speechless.

"Let's go. Now!" I said sharply, although under different circumstances I think I would have obliged the lady—at least once.

And then she was on me. "You fucking son of a bitch!" she screamed, making me glad I had had the foresight to shut the stairwell door behind me.

I raised my hand to slap her again, and she backed off immediately, a sly smile on her lips.

"The president will hear about this. A Secret Service man trying to rape his son's girlfriend."

I laughed out loud, took her arm, and led her back downstairs without another word or any further resistance. No one had noticed we were missing, and a few minutes later Stanley's news conference was over, and so was the tour.

It was eleven o'clock by the time I had seen Stanley and Olanda safely back to the hotel. I was told that Stone wanted to see me in the morning, not this evening as he had said. I assumed that the president had been as good as his word and had somehow convinced Stone that the world tour could not be canceled.

I took a cab across town to a little restaurant, where I tried to telephone Kazuka at home. There was no answer there, so I tried Amalgamated Press. Kazuka answered the phone on the first ring.

"Nick," she said, and she sounded excited.

"What have you got on those two men?" I asked.

"Nothing. But there is a message for you from a gentleman in Washington."

"David?" I said.

"Yes," Kazuka replied. "He wants you home immediately. It's urgent."

"Anything else?" I said, my mind running to a dozen different possibilities.

"No. He wants you home; that's all." Kazuka hesitated, and I could almost see her sad expression. "I've booked you on a special diplomatic flight. Leaves Tokyo at two this morning."

"Right," I said. "Kazuka—" I started, but she cut me off.

"Don't say anything, Nick darling. If and when you can, come back to me. I love you." And then she hung up.

VI

"YOU'LL HAVE JUST four days before you're to catch up with the presidential party in Cairo," Hawk was saying to me.

I sat across the desk from him in his familiar cluttered office on Dupont Circle, my mind still a bit befuddled at the rapidity of not only switching a few time zones, but coming across the International Date Line as well.

"I thought the president was only going to spend two days in Peking," I said, sitting slightly forward in my chair. Hawk still had not told me why he had called me back from Tokyo so dramatically.

He was shaking his head. "He will remain an extra two days in China. It's safer for him there than, I'm afraid to say, even here in Washington."

Hawk turned and looked out the window at the bleak drizzle that was falling at this moment. He sighed, a gesture I had seen him do only once or twice since I had known him. For a brief instant I felt a pang of fear. Hawk was getting older. And old men were not invulnerable to . . . I did not want to think of Hawk in such final terms, so I brought my mind back to the present as he turned to me.

"The president was a hard man to convince, but I think I can guarantee he'll remain in Peking four days. However, that is all I could get out of him. So you'll have to finish whatever you can in that time and then get to Cairo. Understood?"

I nodded. Convincing the president of anything, I figured, must have been about the toughest thing possible, considering the state I had left him in.

After my call to Kazuka I had gone immediately back to the Imperial Hilton. This time I did declare an emergency to the president's sleepy appointments secretary. I had a scant two hours in which to tell the president what was happening, somehow slip past Stone to retrieve my luggage, pick up my boarding pass at the gate, and make the two-o'clock diplomatic flight.

It took the president nearly ten minutes before he joined me in his living room, and he did not look in the least bit happy. At first I thought his displeasure was directed toward me for waking him up at midnight, but then I realized he was mad about something else.

"What is it, Carter?" he asked almost vacantly but with an angry look in his eyes.

"David Hawk has just ordered me back to Washington," I said without preamble.

"When do you leave?"

"Within two hours. But you should be all right at government center, as long as you make no further public appearances until you board Air Force One for Peking. Whatever Hawk wants, I should be back in time to meet you in Cairo."

The president looked at me for the first time since I had entered the room. "Hawk contacted you here? He wants you back in Washington?"

"Yes, sir," I nodded.

"You have a lead to who is behind all this? You know who sent the Lisbon message?"

I shook my head. "I don't, sir. Perhaps Hawk has some answers. I just thought I would have to let you know I was leaving. I may need you to cover for me with Stone," I added.

The president smiled, almostly sadly. "Quite a little conspiracy we've got going for us here," he said

I returned the smile. "Yes, sir."

The president seemed to hesitate a moment before he said his next words. His shoulders seemed to slump, and he looked at me with an almost pleading expression in his eyes. "It may not be necessary for you to meet me in Cairo, though," he said.

"Sir?"

"I may be canceling the remainder of my tour after Peking. I just don't know at this time."

"I'm sorry—" I started to say, but he waved me off.

"Never mind," he said. "Go to Washington and do what has to be done. If I have no need of you in Cairo I'll contact Hawk."

"Yes, sir," I said. I wanted to stay and talk with him, but he was tired and I was late. As I was about to leave, I remembered the Olanda Williamson thing. I turned back to the president.

"Mr. President," I said.

The president looked at me. "I know all about it," he said.

I must have looked surprised, because he explained, "Stanley told me all about it. But let me assure you I didn't believe a word of it. I know your record. I know the kind of man you are. I also know the kind of man my son is."

There was nothing I could say.

"Don't worry about it, Carter. It's a family thing, nothing more."

Sitting now across from Hawk, half the world away from the president, I wondered if it was just a family thing. Stanley had obviously set me up for the entire incident. Either that or he was one of the biggest, most naïve fools I had ever run into. Either way I was going to have a word with him and his girlfriend as soon as I rejoined the presidential party.

Meanwhile, Hawk was eyeing me. "Troubles, Carter?"

I looked up out of my thoughts. "No, sir," I said. "Just a bit tired."

Hawk shifted the ever present cigar from one side of his mouth to the other, selected a thin file folder from a pile of many on his desk, and opened it. For several moments he scanned the contents of the folder, which I noticed was marked with a thin red band near the top—highest priority—and then he looked up at me.

"Portenjo," he began. "First name Juan. You got his other particulars from your initial query."

"There's more, I hope, sir," I said.

Hawk looked at me impatiently, and I sat back in my chair.

"Quite a character, this Portenjo," Hawk continued. "We had to twist a few arms over the past forty-eight hours, but it was worth it. The man did *not* drop out of terrorist activities after his release from Estoril penitentiary as we first thought, nor were his activities previous to that time confined to local uprisings. On the contrary, Juan Portenjo has been one naughty boy all his life.

"Petty theft at ages five, seven, nine, and eleven. Suspected murder when he was thirteen, again when he was fifteen, and a third time when he was sixteen. No arrests or convictions on those suspicions."

Hawk looked up at me. "The Portugese police do not exactly cooperate well with us about their failures," he said. That comment was the closest to humor I had ever heard Hawk utter. But I said nothing, waiting for him to continue.

"Over the past five years Portenjo has been involved in guerrilla wars, radical demonstrations, labor riots, and strikes, all over Europe, Africa, and finally at home in Lisbon.

"Those last activities, the ones in Lisbon, led to his downfall. He was arrested and imprisoned and, after he served his term, was released last year. Then, two months ago, he dropped completely out of sight."

Hawk handed that file across to me and then selected a second file, opened it, and read for a moment before he continued his monologue.

"Akiro Tsukatani, the man you shot and killed in Tokyo, was a radical Communist. So violent, I understand, that even the Zengakuri movement would have nothing to do with him as of last year. I'll spare the details and let you read about him," Hawk said, closing that file and handing it across. "Needless to say, Mr. Tsukatani also dropped out of sight, completely out of sight, two months ago."

Hawk selected a third file folder and without opening it, passed it across to me. "Mr. Tsukatani's assistant. A little less violent a character, perhaps, but no less dedicated and deadly."

I held the three files on my lap. "Any connection among the three, sir?" I asked.

Hawk selected the final thin file folder from the pile, opened it, and passed a drawing across to me. It looked almost like a stylized rose with four petals, or perhaps an oddly shaped mushroom of some sort, with four convolutions.

I looked up at Hawk.

"That mark was found tattooed on the inner side of the left wrist of each man you managed to take out. A mark of membership perhaps? A code sign for the Lisbon organization—if there is such an organization?" Hawk shrugged. "Research has had the devil's own time with this thing but has come up with absolutely nothing."

I digested that bit of information for a moment. Hawk was correct, of course. It certainly was no coincidence that three men in two widely separate places in the world, all coming to assassinate a president of the United States, had identical tattoos on their inner left wrists. There was no doubt in my mind that the tattoo signified the Lisbon organization—whatever it was. But if we only knew what the symbol meant or stood for, it might lead us a long way toward ending this.

I looked up again. "Any other connections, sir?" I asked.

Hawk nodded and withdrew a second sheet of paper from the last file folder. "This from computer analysis. A bit tricky, actually. Once again we bent a few regulations to come up with this so quickly, and I'm afraid we might have bent a few computers."

I looked questioningly at my boss, but he was going to take his time, as usual.

"Once we had IDs on these three characters and had figured out from the tattoos that they were in all likelihood connected, and in all likelihood something happened to them in common that caused them to drop out of sight two months ago, we tried to trace their movements of two months ago."

I was perplexed, and it must have shown on my face, because Hawk shifted his cigar impatiently.

"Bear with me, Carter. This one piece of information cost AXE upwards of a quarter of a million dollars. We still haven't gotten all the bills. I hope it's worth it.''

Again I said nothing, but this time I was stunned to speechlessness. AXE had never spent a quarter of a million dollars on anything before. AXE just did not have that kind of money—at least, I didn't think it had.

''With the positive IDs, their photographs, and the probable date of their movements, we ran computer surveys for every major, and a good many minor, points of entry to countries all over Europe, the Orient, and a few other places that were such wild guesses I won't even mention them.''

I was even more stunned.

''And of course we found that all three of those men were in Lisbon near that time. But even more interestingly, we also found that all three entered West Germany on the same day six weeks ago. We don't know where in Germany they went. But we do know they all entered Germany on the same day.''

''So there is a Lisbon organization. There is a highly organized plot to kill President Magnesen. And they are not going to give up.''

''Exactly,'' Hawk said, handing me the last file. ''Read those, and then return them to me before you leave this office. You'll be leaving for Lisbon within''—he paused a moment to glance up at the wall clock—''two and a half hours.''

I sighed.

''Find the connection between Portenjo and the

two Japanese and their friends. Find out what the
red tattoo means. And put an end to these damned
plots to kill our man.''

VII

LISBON IS AN ancient city built on steep hills. Located on the bay into which the Tagus River flows, the city of almost nine hundred thousand people was listed in all the tourbooks as a major Atlantic seaport, as well as a thriving transoceanic airline center.

Lisbon is all that and very much more, however, as I knew first hand.

During World War II, the city served as a clearing house for Nazi intelligence and counterintelligence networks. Those years had left their stamp on the city, which now probably contained more intelligence agents per square mile than even Washington, D.C.

Often my assignments had taken me to this city, and over the years I had developed an aversion for the place. Everyone here fancied himself a spy. Everyone seemed to play the game, which more than once has become time consuming for me. It's like trying to run through a crowd and make good time. And time was something I had precious little of on this trip.

I took a cab directly to my hotel, the Conrad Hilton Lisbon—a little higher class of hotel than I normally stay at on assignment, but I had wanted it that way this time, and Hawk had agreed with me.

The Lisbon organization had mounted two very nearly successful attempts on the president's life in two widely separated places. That meant their organization was well run and probably well financed. It also meant that there was probably at least one observer in the crowds during the attempts.

If that was the case, then the Lisbon organization also knew me, at least by sight. I was the one who always spoiled their well-laid plans.

When I showed up in Lisbon, I hoped it would cause them confusion. What was a presidential Secret Service man doing here in Lisbon? With any luck I was hoping they would be confused enough to try to pick me up, or perhaps kill me. If and when that happened, I'd have a chance to follow the lead all the way to the top.

My reasoning was that by checking into the Hilton in Lisbon, I could make just a big enough show of it, that if anyone were watching, they'd be sure to notice me.

Hawk had agreed. The desk clerk whom I stood before at this moment seemed an agreeable sort, too. "Señor Carter, welcome please to the Lisbon Hilton," he said smoothly with a toothy grin, as he handed me a registration card.

I returned the smile. "Thanks," I said. "I've just come from the Hilton in Tokyo, and I liked it so much I had to stay at the Hilton while I'm here." I quickly filled out the card and handed it back to him.

"How long will you be staying as our guest, señor?" the clerk asked, as he rang for the bellhop.

I shrugged. "That depends on my business."

The bellhop came across the lobby to us. The clerk handed him my key and nodded slightly toward me. "Show señor Carter to his room," he said.

The bellhop took my bag and half-bowed to me. "This way, señor."

I shook my head and handed him a five-dollar bill. "Take my bags upstairs. I'll be in the bar," I said.

"Very good, señor," the bellhop said. Pocketing the bill, he turned and headed toward the elevators as I ambled casually across the lobby and entered the large, well-lit, and very well-appointed bar.

It was shortly after noon, Lisbon time, and I was hungry, so I ordered lunch with my drink, then sat back and relaxed. I did not want to rush this too much. If anyone was here to greet me, I wanted them to have plenty of time to get set.

I was sure that once I went snooping around Juan Portenjo's apartment—which would, of course, be clean—the organization would have no doubts about me whatever.

The president's handpicked man . . . stopped two assassination attempts . . . now poking around Portenjo's apartment . . .

They would have to take me out—there was no doubt about it. I could feel the adrenaline beginning to pump into my veins.

For a brief moment I thought about Kazuka Akiyama back in Tokyo. It was doubtful that I would be back there this time, but the thought of Tokyo triggered something else in my mind.

Every case I've ever been on has been something like a jigsaw puzzle—a confusing jigsaw puzzle, sometimes so confusing that I do not even know the size or extent of it.

My first step in most cases, as in working on any puzzle, is to come up with the boundaries. As I gathered up the pieces and tried to fit them together I began to get other ideas, or at least a feeling for what the entire puzzle looked like.

This time the puzzle was big. It covered the entire world, or at least the world the president would be touring. Already some of the pieces were beginning to fit together. But there were still pieces of the puzzle that didn't seem to fit anywhere.

Item: Olanda Williamson. She was no more a magazine writer than I was. At least, that was my gut feeling about her, although her background did seem to check out.

Item: Again Olanda Williamson. Why make a pass at me in Tokyo? It didn't make sense.

Item: The president's son, Stanley. He had obviously wanted to talk to me that night, but he didn't. Why?

Item: Again the president's son. Why did he tell his father I had tried something funny with his girlfriend? And why was he so against his father's going on this world trip?

None of those pieces, if they *were* pieces to this puzzle, seemed to fit anywhere.

And then there was Derrick Stone, I told myself as I paid for my lunch and left the hotel. When I rejoined the presidential party in Cairo he would have plenty of questions for me—questions I was going to have to come up with plausible answers for. My absence would have increased his already almost unbearable suspicion of me. His suspicion pointed to the possibility that he was a key member in the Lisbon organization, the leak from the Washington end. But that was one speculation I was finding hard to swallow, even though he always seemed to be in my way and seemed so inefficient at stopping assassination attempts.

Without trying to hide anything, I took a taxi directly across town to the waterfront district. The address I had been given by research in Washington for Portenjo's apartment turned out to be a ramshackle warehouse on the first floor with a half dozen dingy apartments on the second story.

I dismissed the cab and went upstairs to a narrow, dimly lit, filthy corridor. The smells of frying beans and greasy meat were almost sickening.

Somewhere behind one of the doors, a baby was crying.

The last door toward the rear of the building was the one listed as Portenjo's apartment. I knocked once, stepped to one side, and waited with my right hand near my open coat.

A moment later the door opened a crack and an old woman, clad only in a filthy house dress, with no shoes, peered out at me.

"*Si?*" she said.

Quickly in Portugese, I told the woman that I was looking for Juan, who was an old friend of mine.

The woman looked at me as if I were crazy, then closed the door. A moment later a man opened it. He was large, much bigger than me, and wore filthy, baggy trousers, rope-soled shoes, and a gray T-shirt with the sleeves cut off.

"What do you want?" he said to me in English.

"Juan Portenjo," I said.

The man shook his head. "You got the wrong place," he said. He started to close the door, but I moved forward quickly and with my shoulder to the door pushed it all the way open.

The man, caught off-balance, stepped back and began to raise his fists toward me, but when I pulled out Wilhelmina and pointed it at him, his entire manner suddenly changed. His attitude switched dramatically from one of burly roughness to one of peasantlike groveling at a master's feet.

"Please forgive me, señor," the man said, switching back to Portugese.

"Juan Portenjo," I said again.

The man started to shake his head, so I reached up and pulled back the ejector on my Luger, snapping a round into the firing chamber and cocking the hammer. The man blanched.

"Juan Portenjo," I repeated.

"Not here . . . " the man stammered. "He is not here. No longer."

"Where is he?" I asked, noticing out of the corner of my eye that the woman was cowering against the far wall.

"I don't . . . " the man started to say. I raised the Luger a little higher so that it was pointed directly between his eyes.

"Madre Dios . . . " the man mumbled, crossing himself. "Señor, I swear to the Virgin Mary, I do not know where Juan is."

"How long ago was he here?" I continued.

"Six weeks, maybe two months ago," the man said, almost choking on the words. "I swear to you."

I was about to press him for an exact date, when something in the expression in his eyes suddenly changed. In that moment, something hard hit me on the back of my head, and a flash of light popped in my brain. I realized that I had stupidly remained with my back to an open door.

I must have been out for only a few seconds, because a moment later I was conscious that I was lying on the floor, a terrific pain in the back of my head. Someone smelling of cheap whiskey grabbed my shoulders and dragged me all the way into the room, and a moment later the door was closed and I could hear the latch running home.

Two men were talking rapidly in Portugese, and the woman was moaning and half-crying. I was able to pick out enough of what they were talking about to hear the name Maria Oeirés. Something about how Maria should have to be warned.

Someone wearing thick, heavy-soled shoes walked over to where I lay and I tensed every muscle in my body as one foot came back and the man kicked me in the side.

I rolled over, groaning as if in great pain, which wasn't far from the truth. Through half-closed eyes, I watched as the man I had questioned came across the room, bent down, and quickly searched me.

The man who had kicked me was pointing my gun in my general direction. He was a large man, even larger than the other man, but he was dressed in rough-cut and very clean seaman's garb.

Neither of the men used names, but when the man who had just searched me stood up, he handed my wallet to the man with my gun. They had failed to find Hugo, my stiletto, or Pierre, the tiny gas bomb. So I still had a chance.

The man with my gun flipped open my wallet and started going through the ID cards that showed me as Nick Carter, American Secret Service attached to the presidential detail. This seemed to excite him so much that he temporarily forgot about me.

It was all the opening I needed. In an instant I had Hugo in my right hand. I tensed my muscles and shot up, driving the stiletto between the man's ribs and into his heart.

There wasn't even time for a facial reaction on the man, as he dropped like a felled ox.

The man I had questioned, however, leaped for the door. In an instant I was on my feet, and I slammed my fist into the side of his head as he was fumbling with the latch. He, too, went down like a steer in a slaughterhouse.

All through this the old woman had been cowering in the corner of the room, mumbling and half-crying. I collected Hugo, wiped it off, and slipped it back in its case, and then I retrieved and holstered my Luger.

A quick search of both men showed very little unusual. Neither of them had the curious tattoo on the inner left wrist.

The back of my head was still sore, which was fully explainable when I searched the larger man's jacket pockets and came up with the solid-oak belaying pin he had hit me with.

Turning my attention now to the woman, I pulled her away from the wall and sat her roughly down on the ancient, lopsided couch. I had no intention of hurting her, but she didn't know that. Her eyes were rolling in their sockets, and spittle drooled down from the corners of her mouth as she mumbled something about "Jesus the savior," who would protect her.

Very carefully, and in my best and most formal Portugese, I told the woman that death and destruction would come to her family and that her soul would burn in the everlasting fires of hell if she did not cooperate with me.

She looked up at me, and then down at the two men lying on the floor. "My husband," she stammered. "Is he . . . dead?"

I shook my head. "No. He will be all right. But the other man is dead."

"Merciful God in heaven," the woman wailed, wringing her hands.

"Who is Maria Oeriés?" I said sharply.

The woman looked up at me and through her tears, mumbled, "Juan's girlfriend."

"Juan . . . " I started to say, but then changed my mind. She had heard me, though.

"Yes . . . yes," she cried. "Juan is our son. Merciful God in heaven help us."

I suddenly felt very sorry for this old woman and the man I had knocked down by the door. They were the parents of Juan Portenjo, but they were innocent. They knew nothing about the Lisbon plot. The other man, however, was most likely one of the organization's cleanup men, sent here to make sure neither of them talked to me. If he had been too late to stop me, he would have killed them.

I was more gentle with the woman. "You have not seen Juan in two months?"

She nodded. "He is a good boy," she cried. "He is in with bad people."

I smiled sadly. "What bad people?" I asked.

She shook her head. "I do not know," she said. "Maria is one of them. A bad woman. Bad . . . "

"Where is Maria?" I asked. "Where can I find her?"

The woman looked up into my eyes. "I will tell you, and then you will stop my son from whatever it is he is about to do. Promise me on God's mercy . . . promise you will do that?"

"Yes," I nodded. I did not have the heart to tell her that at this moment her son was laying in the morgue in Honolulu.

The old woman gave me the address of Maria Oeriés and, having recovered somewhat, told me to go. She and her husband would take care of the body.

Reluctantly I left their apartment. A few blocks away I found myself a cab, giving the driver the name of my hotel.

There was no doubt in my mind that the woman and her husband could get rid of the body. But I was worried about who would be calling on them next.

I could not call the Lisbon police and ask them to protect the couple, because even if they could, their movements would tip off the Lisbon organization that I knew even more than they suspected and had gone to the local authorities with it. This would do nothing more than drive them deeper underground. They would be making fewer mistakes, and my job would be that much more impossible.

Back at my hotel, I paid the cabby and hurried up to my room. Inside, I quickly checked my two suitcases. Both had been opened and searched. That really didn't matter, because anything of importance was either carried on my person or disguised as part of the suitcase frame, hinges, or handles.

The Lisbon organization knew I was here. I would have to keep on my toes from now on.

I quickly changed clothes, cleaned and oiled my stiletto, and then left via the fire stairs at the end of the corridor.

After taking three cabs and two buses and walking for more than an hour, I had covered most of Lisbon and, in an extremely roundabout fashion made my way to the apartment of Maria Oeriés, in the Alfama quarter near the cathedral.

VIII

IT WAS NEARLY six o'clock by the time I took up my position across the street from the building in which Maria Oeriés lived. I wanted to watch the front door for at least an hour before making my move.

If Portenjo's parents were unsuccessful in removing the dead man from their apartment unnoticed, or if someone else from the Lisbon organization had been acting as a backup observer there, it was safe to bet that they would be sending someone around to Maria's apartment.

There were only a couple of other people in the

small café where I waited, so I was easily able to get a small table by the window. As I sipped my hot, sweet, thick Portugese coffee, I was able to watch the front door of the ancient but well-kept four-story building across the street.

How did Maria Oeriés fit into all this? I asked myself. Portenjo's mother evidently believed that Maria had been a bad influence on her son, but that could have been nothing more than a mother's concern for her son's welfare. Every mother wanted her son to marry a nice girl, someone he could settle down with to raise a family.

On the other hand, the old woman had called Maria Oeriés "bad." Did that mean bad like criminal? Bad like wanton? Bad like what?

I shrugged. I would be finding out soon enough, I hoped.

For the next hour I sat sipping my coffee and waiting, but no one suspicious entered or left the apartment building. I signaled for the waiter, paid my check, and went outside. Across the street I entered the building and looked at the mailboxes in the narrow lobby. Maria Oeriés was listed, as Portenjo's mother had said she would be, for apartment 4B, on the top floor.

I avoided the creaking, iron-cage elevator and took the stairs, silently but swiftly. In a couple of minutes I was standing outside the door to her apartment, listening. I could hear soft music from within, but nothing more. A moment later I knocked.

To say that I was surprised when the door was opened would be the understatement of the year. I was flabbergasted. The woman standing at the open door in a thick terrycloth robe was easily one of the most beautiful women I had ever seen. She was of medium height, about five-five or five-six, weighed perhaps 115 pounds, and was built as a woman should be built—at least as far as I could tell with the robe wrapped tightly around her.

But her face was almost the best. If ever there could have been a cross between Elizabeth Taylor and Brigitte Bardot in a Portugese package, this young woman was it.

All that, I saw in the space of an eyeblink, and in the next moment a dozen questions crowded into my mind.

If this was Maria Oeriés, and she was Portenjo's girlfriend, what had she seen in him? My recollection of him from Honolulu did not fit the kind of a man I would expect to see by this woman's side.

And if this was Maria Oeriés, and Portenjo's mother was correct that she was a bad woman, I was very interested in finding out: bad how?

"Señorita Oeriés?" I asked, smiling slightly.

The woman nodded slowly. She seemed frightened; at any moment she might bolt.

"I come from Juan Portenjo," I said. "I'd like to talk to you about him."

She stared at me for a long moment, her eyes widening and her mouth coming open to reveal perfect teeth. Then she burst into tears, swiveled, and rushed into the apartment, leaving the door open.

I hesitated a moment while glancing either way down the corridor—no one was there—and then went into the apartment, closing and locking the door behind me.

The apartment was a tiny efficiency unit, in one room. The kitchenette was partitioned off from the room by a sliding door, and another door to my right evidently led to the bathroom. A privacy screen across the room from me barely hid a large double bed, and from where I stood I could see Maria's legs from the knees down, sticking out from her robe as she lay on her belly sobbing.

I quickly checked the bathroom, the kitchen, and the large closet-cabinet before I turned back to the woman on the bed. She was still crying, her shoulders racked with her sobs.

We were alone in the apartment. If anyone from the Lisbon organization had found out what had gone on earlier today, they would have been here by now. And since they were not, I suspected I would have a little time—a suspicion that was totally wrong.

I gingerly sat on the edge of the bed and reached over to rub Maria's back between her shoulderblades, massaging also the base of her neck.

Slowly her sobs subsided, and for several minutes she just lay there as I continued to rub her back and neck.

"Where is Juan?" I asked finally, keeping my voice as soft and gentle as possible.

"I don't know," she said, her words muffled by the pillow. "I don't know."

Neither Juan Portenjo's name nor his picture had been published in any paper in connection with the assassination attempt on President

Magnesen in Honolulu. So why was Maria crying now? If it was because Portenjo was dead, that meant she was a part of the Lisbon organization and therefore privy to that knowledge.

"When did you see him last?" I asked, continuing my massaging.

"Eight weeks ago," she said.

"I heard he might be dead," I started, but Maria suddenly flipped around in the bed and sat up, her face a mask of horror.

"No!" she wailed. "They said he lived—" She broke off.

I grabbed her face in both my hands. "They?" I said. "Who are they? What do you know about them?"

She struggled against my grasp. "Leave me alone!" she screamed. "Go away from here."

I let my hands slip down to the side of her face, so that my thumbs were positioned below and to either side of her jaw, and I began to apply pressure. Instantly she stiffened, the screams choking off, her eyes bulging nearly out of their sockets.

I intensely dislike causing pain to any woman, especially a woman so beautiful as Maria Oeriés, but I hate even more a murderer, especially an assassin.

"Maria," I said softly, releasing the pressure on her neck, "I want answers."

She tried to pull away from me, but I held her firmly. "I can't," she mewed.

"You must," I insisted, increasing the pressure on my thumbs slightly.

She stiffened again, and her eyes rolled in terror.

"They'll kill me!" she managed to gasp.

I took my hands away, and she lay back down on the bed, massaging her neck, as the tears again began to slip down her cheeks. In her struggles the front of her robe had parted slightly revealing her thighs and a good portion of her breasts.

I was sitting next to her on the bed, and I leaned over her now to look directly into her eyes.

"Juan was involved in an attempt to kill a prominent American," I said. "But he was not successful. He was killed in the attempt."

I let that sink in for a moment before I continued. She was crying now, silently, the tears streaming down her cheeks.

"I'm sure they will not hesitate to kill you, Maria, if they think you are cooperating with me. But if you don't answer my questions now, I'll leave and spread the word that you did talk to me."

A look of panic flashed across her face.

"If you do cooperate with me, I'll get you out of here. I'll guarantee your protection. You'll be safe. And the people responsible for Juan's death will be caught."

She reached out and touched my arm. When she spoke her voice was choked with emotion. "They told me that Juan was still alive. That he was hiding. That he would come back to me."

"What else did they tell you?" I asked gently as she moved a little closer to me. Her movement caused her robe to open in the front even more, and what I was seeing was very nice.

"They told me that someone would be coming

here to question me," she said, a huskiness coming to her voice.

"Did they mention any names?"

She shook her head and raised her left knee. The robe fell all the way open now, so that she was completely nude in the front. Her body perfectly matched her gorgeous face, and I was suddenly having difficulty in concentrating.

"Who are they?" I asked again, taking a deep breath. Sometimes Yoga breathing exercises help calm me down. This time they weren't doing much good.

She shook her head. "I don't know. Juan had his friends; I had mine. A couple of months ago he took off on business, as he called it. He said that he'd be back soon and that he would have enough money for us to go away."

"And you've heard nothing else from him?"

"Nothing," she said. "But two days ago I got a phone call. It was a man who said that he knew where Juan was and that Juan would be safe as long as I said nothing to anyone. He said someone would probably be coming to question me, but I was to answer nothing."

"Or?" I said.

For a moment she looked quizzically at me, but then the understanding dawned on her. "Or they would kill me and Juan," she said.

I turned away thoughtfully for a moment. Either this woman was telling me the truth or she was one of the finest actresses I had ever run into. She touched my arm, bringing me back to the present.

"I'm frightened," she said in a small voice.

I reached out and caressed her cheek with the back of my hand, and she snuggled even closer to me, reached out with both hands, and drew me down on top of her.

Her body was soft and warm, and she smelled faintly of a fresh bath and powder. She hooked a leg around one of my legs and pulled me all the way on top of her and then kissed me passionately, her tongue darting around my lips.

The lady was lonely, I told myself. Lonely and beautiful. And she had answered my questions, at least to this point. But I had many more to ask—a lot tougher questions, which might take a little pursuasion. Like the names of Juan's friends and what he had done during the months before his disappearance.

First, however, I told myself, I wanted to see just how far she would go with her little act, if it was an act.

Soon her robe was off, I was undressed, and we were making love, her incredible breasts crushed against my chest each time I moved against her.

The moment after we were finished, I felt her body stiffen. Her arm flashed over her head, and she grappled for something beneath her pillow. I was off-balance on one knee and one elbow; otherwise, she would not have come as close as she did.

I flipped completely over as her hand came up, and the straight razor, clutched tightly in her little fist, flashed in the dim light. The sharp blade raked across my outstretched arm, barely nicking the skin but drawing blood, and in the next instant I had her wrist and was bending it forward.

At the point where I thought her wrist would surely break, Maria finally let out a little cry, dropped the razor, and tried to knee me in the groin. I easily fended off the blow, let go of her wrist, and flipped the razor across the room.

"Nice try, sweetheart," I said. "And now for the answers I came for."

She was on me in an instant, her long, well-manicured fingernails raking across my already cut arm.

I slapped her hard across the face, instant red coming to her cheek, but she struggled up for me again, so I grabbed her arm just above the elbow and applied firm pressure. She yelped in pain and flopped back on the bed, a combination of hate and fear in her features.

Holding her down, I reached out with my other hand and picked up the phone on the night table. Before the operator had a chance to come on the line, I spoke into the mouthpiece, in Portugese.

"The federal secret police," I said. "And please hurry."

"No!" the girl shouted as the operator came on the line.

"Your call please?"

"Never mind," I said, and hung up the telephone, then turned to look down at the deeply frightened woman. "And now for some straight answers, or I'll let your own government deal with this."

The Portugese federal secret police is probably the most ruthlessly efficient agency of its kind in the world. It is small in number but very large in influence among its own people. There are very few in Portugal who do not know and fear its force.

Maria Oeriés was completely cowed now by my threat, and she began mumbling and babbling about her instructions to kill me.

"And when you had accomplished that, what next?" I asked.

She looked up at me with her liquid brown eyes and shook her head. I again reached for the telephone, and her eyes darted from my outstretched hand back to the firm expression on my face.

"I was to call a number," she said half-hysterically, shaking her head back and forth. "Someone would come and take your body—take you away and clean up."

I picked up the phone and handed it to her. "Call them," I said.

She shrank away from the phone.

"Call them or I'll call the police," I said. I could hear the operator asking for the number.

Maria finally reached out, took the phone, and gave the operator the number. A few moments later someone evidently answered, because she stiffened and then nodded her head. "Yes," she said, and then she handed the phone back to me.

I put the receiver to my ear in time to hear the click at the other end, and then nothing.

"A man or a woman?" I asked as I hung up the phone.

"A man," she said, and then she rolled over and buried her face in the pillow and began to sob again.

Within a couple of minutes I was up and dressed, my Luger in hand, a round in the chamber, the safety off. When the knock came at the door I snapped around to Maria, who had jumped up and was standing next to the bed, tying the robe tightly around her. The tears were still streaming down her cheeks, and she was so frightened that I wondered if she was going to be able to walk.

The knock came again, and I silently motioned for her to answer the door, as I took up position behind it.

On the third knock, Maria opened the door. From where I was standing I could see through the hinge line of the door a tall, redhaired woman standing in the corridor, holding what looked like a silenced .32-caliber Beretta.

I started to move forward to push Maria out of the way, but the unmistakable low plop of a silenced gun being fired sounded twice, and Maria crumpled where she stood, jamming the door shut with her body.

For what seemed like ten minutes, but was more like ten seconds, I struggled to get Maria's body out of the way. I yanked open the door and rushed into the corridor, Wilhelmina at the ready.

The corridor was empty, but a moment later I noticed that the elevator indicator showed that the iron cage was descending. Without thinking I leaped down the stairs, taking them three at a time, easily beating the ancient elevator to the ground floor.

When the iron doors opened and I looked into an

empty elevator, I realized with a sinking feeling that I had fallen for one of the oldest tricks since elevators had been invented. While I was chasing an empty elevator, the redhaired woman had leisurely made her way down a set of back stairs or the fire escape.

By now she was long gone, surely enjoying her joke on me.

A couple of people in the lobby were backing away from me because of the gun in my hand, so I hurried back upstairs to see if there was anything I could do for Maria before the Portugese police arrived. I did not want to be held up here any longer than need be—especially in a Portugese prison, in which I was sure my chances of survival were very slim.

Maria was still alive, but she was losing blood fast when I arrived back at her apartment and laid her on the bed.

I got a couple of bath towels and tried to stop the flow of blood as best I could, but even an amateur in first aid could easily see that the woman would soon be dead. One of the bullets had caught her just below the sternum, and the other had penetrated low in her abdomen. She must have been in intense pain.

She was trying to speak to me, so I leaned over and put my ear near to her mouth.

"Wiesbaden," she said, the word barely audible. "Two months ago . . . Wiesbaden . . . Germany."

"Juan and his friends were in Wiesbaden two months ago?" I said.

She was barely able to nod.

It fit with what Hawk had found out. Juan and the two Japanese terrorists had entered Germany two months ago. They had evidently gone to Wiesbaden.

"Where in Wiesbaden?" I asked.

"Max Schiller Strasse," she managed to say. "Number 17."

"Who else was there?" I asked urgently, but a spasm of intense pain racked her delicate little body, and I knew she could not last much longer.

"Red fist . . . " she breathed. "Red fist . . . four fingers." And then she died.

Death is never pretty, no matter in what form it comes or to whom. But in the case of Maria Oeriés, one of the most beautiful women I had ever known, it was especially hideous.

I covered her pain-contorted face with the edge of the blanket and then left the apartment as sirens sounded in the distance.

I quickly found the back stairs that the redhaired woman had probably used to make her escape, and within a couple of minutes I was out on the street, nonchalantly walking away.

Number 17 Max Schiller Strasse in Wiesbaden, Germany, the girl had told me. And the tattoo on the inner wrists of Portenjo and the two Japanese depicted a red fist—the international sign of power.

But she had said the fist had four fingers, as if that had some significance. What did it mean?

IX

EL KAHIRAH, AL-QAHIRA, or Cairo, depending upon your language, shimmered in the intense heat of the noonday sun as I was passed immediately through customs on my diplomatic passport. I hailed a taxi for downtown.

I had sent off a coded telegram to Hawk at Amalgamated Press before I left Lisbon, and the reply had been handed to me at the airline terminal here in Cairo just moments ago.

Now riding in the wheezing Citroën taxi toward the center of the capital of Egypt, I opened the telegram and read it.

It was in plain language, very simple, and straight to the point. In my telegram, I had briefly told Hawk what had happened in Lisbon and asked him to cover for me with Stone and the presidential party. He had complied.

EVERYTHING COVERED BOTH ENDS STOP REJOIN COMPANY STOP YOU ARE EXPECTED STOP.

The presidential party had spent four days in Peking, where everything had gone smoothly. They would spend today and tomorrow morning here in Cairo and then would head to Moscow. In the Soviet Union there would be no trouble, I was sure, but here in Cairo I was equally as sure that another attempt would be made on the president's life. Before that happened, I needed some answers from Stanley Magnesen and his girlfriend, Olanda Williamson.

"Welcome back," Derrick Stone said dryly as I slumped down in the chair across the desk from him.

Wherever the president went, the Secret Service usually had its operating headquarters a very short distance from the presidential suite. In this case Stone's office also served as his sleeping quarters and was a room two doors down from the president's in Prime Minister Mohammed El-Akbar's palatial home.

Normally, having the president's Secret Service in attendance at a government leader's private home would have been in bad taste, but the Egyptian leader had insisted on it because of the attempted assassinations in Honolulu and Tokyo.

"We will all feel safer for you, Mr. President," the Egyptian leader had said. And Akbar's own contingent of guards had been doubled.

Stone looked uncomfortable behind the ornate desk that had been moved in for him.

"Everything went well in Peking?" I said conversationally.

Stone nodded. "It was the first vacation I've had in two years," he said.

"You should have it easy in Moscow the day after tomorrow as well," I said, and Stone nodded absently. "But what about today and tomorrow?" I asked. "Has his schedule changed?"

Stone shook his head. "Today is all right. He'll be spending all his time right here closeted with the Egyptian Prime Minister and his advisors. We're to do nothing."

"But . . . " I let it trail off.

"But tomorrow is a different story. Tomorrow they will be making a tour of the pyramids of Giza and the great sphinx southwest of here."

"It'll happen then," I said, half to myself.

"There will be another attempt?" he asked, sitting forward. For the first time, his facial expression was animated.

I nodded. "Most likely they'll try again," I said. If Stone was the leak who was informing the Lisbon organization of the president's moves, it did not matter any longer that he knew I was on to something. Half of Lisbon knew it by now.

If it was Stone, however, and I doubted it, there was a possibility he would make a mistake.

But Stone sighed and sat back in his chair. "They," he said softly. "Another attempt." He smiled and shook his head, then stared at me for several long seconds. "I was told to keep clear of you, not to ask any questions, not to crowd you, but I don't know if that's possible."

"What do you want to know, Stone?" I asked, lighting one of my specially blended cigarettes.

Stone sat forward again. "First of all, who the hell are you?"

I smiled. "Just who I seem to be. The president's handpicked personal bodyguard. Nothing more."

"Bullshit," Stone said, but then he shrugged. "But I guess we'll have to leave it at that."

I nodded.

"You said 'they' will try again. Who are 'they'?"

"I don't know yet. Some organization—backed by whom, I don't know, and for what exact purpose, I don't know—wants the president dead."

"The tattoo?" Stone asked.

I nodded.

"I expect that if another attempt is made and we can stop it, the assassin will be tattooed."

"*If* we can stop it," Stone repeated. "Why don't you talk with the president? He evidently listens to you. Make him quit this insanity and return to Washington."

I shook my head. "For once I agree with you, Stone, but I cannot. With the president back in Washington, we'll never get to the bottom of this.

And sooner or later they'll try again—maybe successfully.''

"So our president is being used as a decoy.''

"As frightening as that sounds,'' I said, "I'm afraid you are right.''

Stone stared at me again for a long time. "Where were you when we were in Peking?''

"I can't tell you that,'' I said.

"Why?''

"I can't tell you that, either.''

Stone was frustrated. He was about to speak again, but I held him off.

"Look,'' I said. "You just do your job and let me do mine as best I can. If and when I can tell you anything—anything at all that will help you protect the president—I'll tell you. Meanwhile, even if I did tell you where I was and what I had been doing it wouldn't help one bit in protecting Magnesen.''

Stone looked away for a long moment, and when he returned his gaze to me he seemed almost sad. "There is a leak somewhere here, and you suspect me.''

I shook my head. "I did suspect you, just as I suspected everyone else. But not now.''

Stone sighed again deeply. "What's the next step?''

"Stanley Magnesen,'' I said, and Stone nearly fell off his chair.

"Are you crazy?'' he said through clenched teeth.

"Don't jump to conclusions,'' I snapped. "Now where is Stanley?''

"In his room. He's come down with a cold or the flu or something. The doctor has him on penicillin and wants him to remain in bed for the rest of the day and tonight."

I nodded. "And Olanda Williamson?"

"A shopping tour this afternoon. The party this evening."

"Here?" I asked.

Stone nodded. "About eight hundred people invited. Every one of them personally vouched for by Akbar himself, who wouldn't let his grandmother in if he figured she'd be carrying a hat pin."

I thought a moment. "All right. I want to be detailed to watch over our Miss Williamson. No one else. Just me."

Stone's eyebrows rose.

"Like I said," getting up, "don't jump to conclusions." And I walked out of Stone's office.

Olanda Williamson was tall, with a model's figure, and somewhat pretty in a New York-plastic sort of way. She could not in any way compare to Maria Oeriés, whose beauty had been classic, but Olanda would turn heads wherever she went.

"What a totally unexpected surprise," she said smoothly when I picked her up at the front gate of the Egyptian palace compound.

I nodded and smiled. "The pleasure is all mine."

"I hope so," she mumbled, and we were off in one of the Mercedes limousines the Egyptian government had provided for us.

We drove into the teeming city, comfortable in

the air-conditioned interior despite the intense afternoon heat, and I began to lecture.

"Cairo, a city of nearly five million people, the capital of Egypt and the largest city in Africa, was founded in A.D. 642.

Olanda looked at me. "Near its site was the ancient Roman city of Babylon and across the river was Memphis, capital of ancient Egypt.' All that from the *Viking Desk Encyclopedia*," she said, and we both laughed.

"Attacked by the crusaders in the twelveth century," I offered.

"Ruled by the Mamelukes from the thirteenth to the sixteenth centuries," she countered.

We laughed again, and the tension between us begin to ease, exactly as I wished. I reached over and took her hand in mine. "What's a nice girl like you doing in a place like this?" I asked, still smiling.

She groaned. "After Tokyo, anything you say or do has got to be for some ulterior motive."

"We all make mistakes," I said. "Even you, telling Stanley."

"Hell hath no fury like a woman scorned," she quipped.

"Seriously," I said, "what are you after? Surely not Stanley."

She peered at me for a long moment, her mouth finally curving into a delicate smile. "No, of course not. I'm on an assignment. But Stanley *is* involved."

I raised my eyebrows but said nothing, waiting for her to continue.

"It's fairly well-known in some circles that Stanley and his father don't get along very well. Stanley has embarrassed the president on more than one occasion. And now with this world tour, which Stanley has publicly spoken out against, the president is hoping to convert his son to his camp."

"Kind of like a father-and-son outing," I suggested.

"Exactly," she said. "Only in this case Stanley is a big boy. Big and exceedingly bright—maybe even bordering on genius. Not a good person to have at your throat but someone who would be a great asset to a president on the university circuit."

"The president wants to use his own son politically?" I said.

Olanda laughed out loud. "My, my, aren't we naïve?" she said. "It's done all the time, Nick."

"And where do you fit into all this?"

"A publisher I'm not at liberty to disclose just yet wants an in-depth piece on Magnesen the younger versus Magnesen the elder. It'll make good copy all the way around. Human interest— we've got a family, the first family, at odds with itself. Politics—what the president is trying to do is magnificent, but his son's objections are penetrating and highly valid."

"And now an added bonus," I said. "Two attempts on the president's life. Should make for exciting reading."

"That's not fair," Olanda snapped.

"But true nevertheless," I insisted, and she nodded.

We were silent for a while then, as we entered the downtown section.

"Where would you wish to be dropped off, Miss Williamson?" the driver asked in a very British accent.

"Anyplace where I can do some shopping," Olanda said.

"Very good, madam," the driver said, and Olanda turned back to me.

"And how about you, Nick Carter? How do you fit into all this?"

"Just another Secret Service agent," I said.

"That's not true. But then, I don't suppose you'll tell me anything about yourself. This is a one-way conversation." She lay back in the seat, stared up at the car's ceiling, and pursed her lips. "Let me see if this is how it goes: Two assassination attempts on President Magnesen. Therefore a plot underfoot to kill our president. The next step would be the conclusion that there is some inside knowledge being spread around. Would have to be, to set the president up this way. The parade route, for instance, had not been announced until an hour before the parade began. Inside information. Which means a leak."

She sat forward and smiled coyly. "And at this moment I'm a suspect. And this little jaunt this afternoon with me is an interrogation session. No doubt you'll be joining me for the party this evening."

I laughed. "Exactly. So don't make any mistakes."

But it did not work out that way for either of us.

The party was to begin at eight o'clock sharp in the palace's main banquet hall. Stone's men had been over the place with a fine-tooth comb under the watchful gaze of Akbar's personal security men.

By seven-thirty that evening I was dressed in my room and about ready to make one more swing through the gigantic hall, when the president's appointments secretary telephoned me that the president wanted to see me immediately. I was due to pick up Olanda Williamson in her quarters at seven-forty five. Stanley was still in bed with the flu. I phoned her room and told her I might be a few minutes late.

The president was dressed in his tuxedo, and when I entered his suite he dismissed his secretary and offered me a glass of champagne, which I accepted.

When we were settled on easy chairs opposite each other, the president put down his glass.

"I want you to leave in the morning, Nick," he said. "I'm pulling AXE off this assignment."

"What?" I said, sitting forward.

"That's right, Carter. You can return to Washington. I'll inform David Hawk of my decision first thing in the morning."

"Mr. President, surely you can't—" I began, but Magnesen abruptly cut me off.

"Don't argue with me Carter," he said. "I'm terminating AXE's involvement in this assignment as of this moment."

"There will be another attempt on your life tomorrow. You do understand that, don't you, Mr. President?" I said softly.

The president's eyes flashed, and then he shook his head tiredly. "I don't believe there will be."

The words were like hammer blows to the center of my skull. The president sounded sure of himself. Too sure about this.

"What have you found out, sir?" I asked, but again the president waved me off.

"I want you to return to Washington tomorrow morning," he said.

My mind was racing in a dozen different directions, and I felt almost like a drowning man clutching at straws. "Mr. President—" I started to say.

"Please, Carter," Magnesen countered, "I'm tired, and I don't think I'd care to match wits with you at this moment. Leave this alone."

I shook my head. I guess I've always stuck my neck on the block. My admirers call it aggressiveness. My enemies call it conceit and a few other more unpleasant things. But I could not leave this alone, not this way. I would have to remain by the president's side at least through tomorrow. Then if nothing happened here, which I sincerely hoped it wouldn't, I would let the president go on to Moscow gladly. I wanted to get to Wiesbaden to check out the address Maria Oeriés had given me.

"Just one day," I said to the president. "Allow me to stay with you through tomorrow. Then you'll be going on to Moscow and I'll leave. I promise."

The president shook his head.

"I don't want to say this, Mr. President, but I feel that I must. I've saved your life twice now, and all I am asking for is one small favor. Allow me to remain with you through tomorrow. That's all.''

For a moment it seemed as if Magnesen were going to explode, and then order me shot, but he finally smiled. ''All right . . . all right. You win. Tomorrow evening you return to Washington.''

Again I shook my head. ''No, sir. Tomorrow I go to Wiesbaden.''

The president's eyes narrowed. ''What are you talking about?''

I quickly explained everything that I had done and learned at my meeting with Hawk in Washington and then during my two days in Lisbon. When I was finished the president no longer looked so good. His complexion had turned from beet-red anger to chalk-white concern.

''There is a Lisbon organization,'' the president said softly.

''It would appear so,'' I answered. ''Tomorrow I'd like to be with you, and then when you go on to Moscow I'll check out the situation in Wiesbaden. If nothing happens tomorrow, and if I find nothing in Wiesbaden, we'll talk again and you will tell me why you were so sure this evening that no more attempts would be made.

The president looked at me for a long time, and at that moment I truly felt sorry for the man. In addition to literally having the problems of the world weighing down on his shoulders, someone now was trying to kill him.

''Agreed,'' he said finally. ''Agreed.''

It was almost eight-thirty by the time I left the

president's suite. When I emerged, several people, including a very anxious appointments secretary, were waiting for the president to head for the party.

I went directly back to my quarters. Suddenly I did not feel very much like going to a party, and yet I wanted more conversation with Olanda. Although her story sounded convincing enough to me, I was still not convinced. I needed a little more time with her to satisfy my own curiosity.

Both birds were killed with one stone.

Olanda was in my quarters when I got there. That was obvious from the moment I walked in the door and saw her shoes in the middle of the sitting-room floor. A few feet beyond the shoes, her dress lay in a crumpled heap, and in the doorway to my bedroom her bra and panties had been thrown down together.

I would not have to go to the party, nor would I miss the opportunity to find out more about Olanda.

X

EVERY MUSCLE IN my body was tense with expectation as we crossed the Nile and sped the short distance southwest of Cairo to the famed pyramids and great sphinx at Giza. I rode in the front seat of the limousine.

It had been the Egyptian minister's suggestion that the American president see the pyramids, one of the seven wonders of the world.

President Magnesen had of course agreed, Stone had nearly had a heart attack over it, and I was nervous. I was almost certain there would be another attempt on Magnesen's life, here in Egypt.

If it did come, it would have to be soon, because the president was leaving on Air Force One for Moscow immediately after this morning's tour.

Stanley Magnesen sat in the back seat, flanked by his father and the Egyptian leader, and as usual his irritatingly high-pitched voice was raised in argument.

From time to time I stole a glance backward. Akbar's expression held a note of amused tolerance, but President Magnesen looked concerned. I wondered if he was concerned about his son's brashness and evident lack of respect for the Egyptian leader or about his own safety, as I was at this moment.

Everything that could be done to ensure the president's safety had been done. The three-mile route from Cairo to Giza, a town of about 710,000, was being continuously patrolled by Akbar's elite guards. The road from Giza to the pyramids had been blocked off to all tourists, and still I had a bad feeling about this.

There would be more than a hundred people at the pyramids, including the presidential party, the Secret Service guards, the Egyptian soldiers, and the hoardes of newspeople who followed the president everywhere.

Ahead of us were two dozen Egyptian soldiers on motorcycles, as well as Derrick Stone and three other Secret Service agents in a Mercedes limousine. Behind us were at least two dozen cars and buses, all filled with newspeople, more American Secret Service agents, and five truckloads of Egyptian soldiers.

It was the heaviest contingent of guards the president had ever had, and yet they were all merely people. Any one of them could have sold out. Any one of them could be a member of the Lisbon organization.

No one knew yet that we were aware of the significance of the red tattoo, so we could not check everyone to see if they had the same mark, without arousing too much suspicion.

My mind was going over every possibility, partly because I wanted to make sure I was leaving nothing to chance and partly because I was using the mental exercise to drown out Stanley's wheedling voice.

Olanda Williamson had left my rooms around three o'clock in the morning, after we had made love, talked for a couple of hours, and then made love again.

Although her physical beauty was no match for that of Maria Oeriés, Olanda Williamson was by far the superior, more accomplished lover. With her long, slender legs and small, firm breasts, she was built for it. And like her almost too-perfect body and sexual technique her story was almost too perfect. During our conversation her details did not change in the slightest. It was almost as if she had carefully rehearsed her lines.

Olanda Williamson seemed too good to be true. But there had been no time to check on her story this morning. It would have to wait until I got to Wiesbaden. And that worried me.

I looked up as we entered Giza. Thousands of people lined the route and waved American flags as the limousine sped by them, never altering its pace.

Stanley was still arguing with the two elder statesmen in the back seat, and now I turned my attention back to them.

If Olanda Williamson, who had not come along this morning, could be called enigmatic, so could her boyfriend, who perfectly fit the mold of the almost radical university thinker. He, too, was almost too perfect to be real.

"I take it, young man, that you approve of neither your father's peace plan nor me as a leader of my people," Akbar said.

"It's not that, Mr. Prime Minister," Stanley said earnestly. "It's that both you and my father are in positions of power, positions from which you could do much good for the world."

"Or much harm," Akbar finished for him, smiling.

Stanley nodded. "Like my father's plan—" he began, but his father cut him off.

"Enough," the president said, but Akbar interceded.

"No . . . no, let the boy continue. It is most entertaining."

Stanley glanced at his father triumphantly and then turned back to the aging Arab leader. "What I'm trying to say, Mr. Prime Minister, is simply this: Before any talk can begin about economic cooperation for world peace, we must first have the elements for peace already at hand."

"And we do not?"

"Of course not, sir," Stanley said. "Take your

country versus the Israelis, for example. Your very dramatic overtures for a peaceful settlement have not convinced everybody. In fact, the controversy could cause violence from other quarters and still not guarantee normal relations with Israel.''

"There will always be violent elements in society. We are acting openly and with total integrity in our struggle for peace.''

"But if peace doesn't come on your terms, you will fight again,'' Stanley said, and I could feel the tension suddenly shoot up in the car. Again President Magnesen tried to stop the discussion, but again Akbar held him off.

"Only as a last resort. We fight only when all negotiations have broken down.''

Stanley smiled. "And if you do fight, where will the peace be then?''

"The same place it was in your Vietnam,'' Akbar said, and Stanley fell silent for a few moments as the presidential convoy entered Giza.

More people were jammed along the convoy's route here, and I studied their faces intently as we sped by. This car was supposedly bomb-proof, which meant that a bomb would have to go off directly alongside the car to do much damage. But that, I mused, could have been arranged.

The first two attempts on Magnesen's life had been professional although fanatical. Any of the people in the crowds could be carrying a bomb.

Stanley's laugh again brought my attention to the three in the back seat. "It's amusing,'' he was saying. "In 1948 you were imprisoned for complicity in the assassination of the Egyptian finance minister, whom you called a diehard anglophile. And then again during the Suez Canal troubles you were making anti-Western statements to the press."

"And yet here we are together?" Akbar finished for him. "The world does change, my boy."

"Yes," Stanley said dryly. "But do people's basic convictions change that much?"

President Magnesen was angry. I could hear it in his voice. "That will be enough," he said sharply to his son.

Stanley started to say something, and the prime minister's voice rose.

"Enough!" he roared, and Stanley finally fell silent.

We left Giza and were waved through the roadblocks. Less than five miles away we could see the mammoth pyramids rising up from the yellow-gray desert. Just beyond them was the great sphinx.

"The impetuousness of youth," Akbar was saying to President Magnesen.

"May I offer my apologies for my son's rash behavior this morning, Mr. Prime Minister," Magnesen said.

"It is entirely unnecessary," Akbar said graciously. "I too as a youth was a radical and a romantic. Today I am the leader of my people. I believe that many great men—men greater than myself—had radical, impetuous beginnings."

"That is very kind of you," President Magnesen said.

Akbar turned to Stanley. "And young man, I

believe that you will find people do change. Some of them for the worse and some for the better. I sincerely seek world peace, every bit as much as your father does. And I believe your father, who is a great leader, may have hit upon the correct solution. Of this we will talk more at a later date."

The caravan had pulled up and parked in a big half circle so that the lead vehicles were already facing back toward town, the presidential limousine less than a hundred yards from the base of the Cheops Pyramid, the largest of the three.

Stone and a half dozen other Secret Service men had immediately surrounded the limousine, and now the doors were being opened for us.

I jumped out of the car on President Magnesen's side and unbuttoned my suit coat so that I would have easier access to Wilhelmina if need be.

The entire place felt like death to me, and I don't think it was merely because we were standing so very close to three ancient tombs. This was death of the more modern variety. I could feel the hairs prickling on my scalp.

Akbar moved around from the other side of the car to join President Magnesen, but Stanley remained in the back seat of the limousine, with the doors closed and the engine running so that the air conditioning would continue to keep the car cool. He looked as if he was pouting.

Akbar led President Magnesen forward toward the Cheops Pyramid, and I took up the rear, to the right of the president, my eyes scanning everyone in the large crowd that had materialized despite the roadblocks.

Besides the newspeople, Akbar's troops, and President Magnesen's own Secret Service, there had to be at least several hundred other people. Most of them seemed to be peasants—desert people, some of them with their donkeys and camels.

I was happy to see that Akbar's soldiers had not only cordoned off a large pathway for Akbar and Magnesen through this crowd, but were also rapidly searching the people and the packs on the animals.

Still, I could not shake the feeling that something was about to happen, and I could see that Stone felt the same way. He was ahead of me, and the president, and was moving slightly to the right, toward where a lone man in the desert robes of a Bedouin stood alongside his camel.

I glanced toward the man and then back at the president, something registering on my unconscious. An instant later I turned back, and the man was gone.

It took me just an instant to see the top of the man's headgear on the opposite side of the kneeling camel. In the next instant the man's arm flew up over his head and something small and dark sailed our way.

"Stone!" I shouted, and then I jumped forward, roughly knocking both President Magnesen and Akbar to the ground, covering their bodies with my own.

The object the man had thrown thumped into the sand at least twenty-five feet away from us, and I turned my head away and buried my face in my arms.

In the next moment the entire world erupted in a gigantic flash, followed by a tremendous roar. The earth leaped as if we were in the middle of an earthquake as something hot and very sharp slammed into my shoulder.

I looked up in time to see the man behind the camel standing up as his arm came back. I scrambled for Wilhelmina, but Stone was kneeling in the sand, his .38 police special Smith and Wesson held in both hands, firing one shot after the other.

The man behind the camel jerked back once, twice—and the third time, he fell. The camel bellowed and jumped up as the hand grenade the man was about to throw exploded, ripping out the frightened animal's side and tearing the man's chest almost completely out of his body.

XI

IT WAS NEARING noon as I turned down Max Schiller Strasse in the Mercedes I had rented at Tem-
pelhof airport in Frankfurt. It had been nearly
twenty-four hours since the third attempt on
Magnesen's life, and now the pain in my shoulder
was a deep, throbbing ache.

Akbar's personal physician had dug the small
hunk of shrapnel from the grenade meant for the
president out of my shoulder, as Stone was hus-
tling Magnesen aboard Air Force One for an early
departure to Moscow.

The Egyptian police, along with a few American

Secret Service agents left behind with me, were clearing up the mess out at Giza and interviewing witnesses.

The press corps had also been hustled off with Magnesen aboard the second air-force aircraft, with threats of bad press for a long time to come because we were hushing up one of the biggest stories they had ever covered. Akbar had cooperated, making Giza and its approaches temporarily off limits.

There had been no time for a positive ID on the assassin, except that he was obviously Arab, and the red fist was tattooed on his inner left wrist.

He was definitely part of the Lisbon organization. They had tried again and failed—but just barely this time.

I had not stuck around Cairo for anything else. Once I was certain of the tattoo and knew that the president was safely on his way, I took the first flight to Germany, and at the airport rented the car for the twenty-mile drive to Wiesbaden.

Number 17 Max Schiller Strasse turned out to be a long, low, dirty yellow brick building on the wrong side of Wiesbaden's tracks—if this lovely city could have such an area.

The building fronted on the narrow street at the city's edge, and I pulled up and parked across from a door marked GESCHÄFTSSTELLE (office). From behind the building I could hear the sounds of a high-powered engine revving over and over again. It was a sound never forgotten, once heard. The last time I had heard it was at the Grand Prix at Monaco. It was the sound of a high-performance formula-one racing car, which fit well with the sign hanging over the front door of the building: OF-FENBACH MOTOREN WERKE, AKG.

Two months ago the Lisbon organization had met here, if Maria Oeriés had been telling me the truth on her deathbed. And two months ago the plot to kill the president of the United States had been given its final touches.

But as I crossed the narrow cobblestoned street and entered the building, I wondered if the trail was too cold by now. Would anything be left here?

"*Darf Ich helfen Sie?*" the matronly receptionist behind the desk asked, looking up as I came in.

"I'd like to speak with Herr Offenbach," I said in German, and I handed her my card. "Nick Carnahan, Amalgamated Press."

"*Moment, bitte,*" the woman said. She got up and disappeared through a door in the back of the very small reception room.

A moment later she returned and guided me through the door, down a short corridor, and into a large, plush office. A huge, rotund man, completely devoid of any facial hair, including eyebrows, rose from an equally massive desk and stretched out his right hand to me.

"Mr. Carnahan?" he said in English, smiling.

I crossed the room to him and took his hand as the receptionist withdrew and closed the door behind her.

"Yes, sir," I said. "Amalgamated Press."

Behind the man, most of the wall was taken up with a large plate-glass window overlooking the remainder of the building, which had once evidently been a factory of some sort. At this moment there were at least a dozen sports and formula racing cars in various stages of completion on the floor, each surrounded by as many as a half dozen mechanics.

Offenbach turned to follow my gaze, and his face broke into a huge grin. "Beautiful, are they not, my little toys?"

"Beautiful," I agreed. "Which is why I am here."

Offenbach turned to me, the smile leaving his face. "And you are from Amalgamated Press?" he asked, looking again at my card.

"Yes."

"Not Ferrari?"

"No, sir."

"I've never heard of Amalgamated Press. What is it?"

"We're a news service, much like the Associated Press or Reuters, but much smaller."

"Office in Frankfurt?"

"Yes."

Offenbach picked up his telephone and a moment later asked his receptionist to telephone the Amalgamated Press office in Frankfurt. He did not put down the phone, but waited for the call to go through.

I had not checked in with our Frankfurt office, which was nothing but a blind number, but the name Carnahan would be a tipoff to the lone woman working at the telephone switchboard that I was on an assignment. It was a code name I had used often.

Our main German office was in Berlin, of course, but we maintained blind numbers in a number of the major German cities, including Frankfurt, Munich, and Bonn.

The connection was made, and Offenbach sat forward to look down at my card. "I have here with me a Nick Carnahan, who claims to be from your office. Do you have such a man on assignment?"

Offenbach nodded, smiled, said, "Thank you," and hung up. "Sorry to have to do that Mr. Carnahan," he said, once again smiling effusively. "But we do have spies in this business, especially so close to an upcoming race. I had to make certain."

"It's quite all right, sir," I said, sighing with relief, and making a mental note to put in a commendation for whoever was at the Frankfurt number today.

"Now what can I do for you specifically? Is it about our Terryll-Ford? Jody Scheckter? Or our pretty little Porsches, which will be running at Spa on Sunday?"

For several long seconds I sat staring at the man, almost as if I were seeing him for the first time. The connection was so obvious that I was surprised I had not made it the moment I knew what 17 Max Schiller Strasse was. Offenbach Motor Works. Racing cars. The Grand Prix at Spa on Sunday.

Today was Thursday. The president would be leaving Moscow sometime on Saturday, arriving in Frankfurt that evening. Sunday morning he was taking a helicopter to Spa, Belgium, for the race. The Lisbon organization, or rather the Red Fist group, had met here two months ago. This attempted assassination would not come as a surprise to me. For the first time I knew the time and place it would occur—sometime during the race at Spa, probably while the president was in his box at the grandstand. It had to be.

"Spa," I finally said. "I'll be covering the race for Amalgamated Press. I'm doing a few pre-race stories now, which is why I came here to see you."

Offenbach beamed. "Then you have come to the correct place, because we are going to win this one."

I nodded. "Perhaps you could show me around," I said, "and answer a few questions."

Offenbach jumped up. "Of course," he said, and then he stopped. He put a finger to the side of his nose and thought a moment, and then his bulbous features spread into a wide grin. "I have something even better for you. Something that will give your story about us some authenticity."

I stood up, a questioning look on my face.

"But first we shall have the tour," he said. "Come with me."

I followed the large man out of his office. Down the short corridor and through a steel door, I found myself on the main floor. The air was torn by sounds of drills, hammers, pneumatic wrenches, and, just outside a set of open garage doors, the incredibly noisy racing engine.

Offenbach had to shout to be heard over the din. "We are preparing three Porsches this year, very similar to last year's Le Mans winner—with a few minor improvements, of course."

"Will all three be run?" I shouted.

We stood near the back wall, the window to Offenbach's office to our right, looking over the workmen frantically making ready the three cars.

"Yes, of course," Offenbach shouted. "There are always mechanical problems. We need to show up in force if we are to have any hopes of winning."

Each of the three cars that would race in Spa in four days was up on blocks, the wheels and body cowling removed, exposing the huge engines, gleaming chromed axles, suspension elements, and tie rods. The exhaust stacks, a huge one for each cylinder, were bunched together at the base as they came out of the manifold and then flared out above the engine like a group of highly polished trumpet bells. An impressive sight.

Offenbach led me over to one of the machines, and I lifted the 35-millimeter camera I had strapped around my neck, but he gently pushed my arm away.

"Please, no photographs. If one were to be published our opposition would glean much information. Too much, perhaps."

"Sorry," I said.

"Not to worry," Offenbach shouted. "The morning of the race you will be my personal guest in the pits and will be allowed to take all the photographs you would like."

"When do you leave for Spa?" I asked.

"Late tonight," Offenbach said. "The exact time and our route, of course, is another secret. We would not want to be hijacked."

I laughed. "Of course not."

Offenbach turned back to look at his cars, and there was obvious pride in his expression. The expression on his face at that moment convinced me that Herr Offenbach had nothing whatever to do with the Lisbon organization. He was just what he seemed to be—the proud owner of Offenbach Motor Works, specialists in designing and constructing formula-one Grand Prix racing machines.

"How many people have you had working on this year's cars?" I asked.

The mechanics working on the Porsche we were standing next to had not looked up when we walked over; they had continued with their work, almost at a feverish pace.

"Not nearly enough," he said. "And the same goes for our team drivers." He looked at me. "Listen, these past two months have been pure hell. More than a dozen of our employees quit on us, some of them men who have worked with me for fifteen or twenty years."

"And the drivers?" I asked, a suspicion growing within me.

"We had five, which was the optimum number. Four of them quit about the same time as the others walked off their jobs. Fortunately for us, we were able to hire two really excellent drivers. But as for the others . . . " He let it trail off and sighed.

A total of sixteen people, four of them drivers, had quit Offenbach two months ago. No coincidence. Nor did I suspect it a coincidence that only two new drivers had been hired, although for the moment I could not figure out why.

With new drivers, probably Lisbon-organization people, now on the payroll, it must have been the plan to take the cars to Spa for the attempt on the president. In all likelihood one of those drivers was the assassin.

But why not hire new mechanics to replace the dozen who quit? Then it struck me. With fewer mechanics, Offenbach would be too harried, too worried, and too busy personally to give much attention or scrutiny to the two men he hired.

Obviously they were top drivers, but what of their backgrounds? Offenbach had his back to the wall and was not about to check on them too closely. Able to hire two drivers almost on top of race day, he was not about to question his good fortune.

It was very smooth. So smooth, in fact, that this place had been selected as the meeting place. But did that mean someone of the original Offenbach crew was part of the Lisbon group?

One other question was bugging me as well. All this apparently pointed to an international organization—Portugese, Japanese, Arab, and now German. But why had the message been sent from Portugal? The radio transmission had been traced to Lisbon, and in all likelihood it had been directed here to Wiesbaden. But why from Lisbon? And why, if it was a Portugese organization, had the meeting two months ago been held here in Wiesbaden?

I was about to ask Offenbach the names of the two new drivers he had hired, when his secretary hurried across from the office door to us.

"Telephone, Herr Offenbach," she said.

Offenbach turned to her. "Yes?" he said peremptorily. "I am busy now."

"*Nein, mein Herr*," she insisted. "It is the International Racing Commission. From Spa. They must speak with you."

Offenbach shook his head in disgust. "Always with the problems just before a race. Forgive me, Mr. Carnahan," he said. "But this may take a while." He looked up and searched the several crews around the three cars until he found the man he was looking for.

"Tell them to wait one moment, please," Offenbach said to his secretary. He led me to the third Porsche, where an older, white-haired man stood apart from the others, his hands on his hips.

The man looked up as we hurried across to him.

"Rudi," Offenbach said, "this is Mr. Carnahan from the Amalgamated Press. He is here to give us some publicity."

"Shit," said the older man, and started to turn away, but Offenbach stopped him with a sharp command.

"Rudi! You will show this gentleman around. It is important to us. Do you understand?"

The man turned back to us, studied my face for a moment, and then shrugged indolently.

"Mr. Carnahan," Offenbach said, "may I present Rudi Gehrmann, my head mechanic. He drinks too much. He swears too much. He is always late for work. And sometimes he plays with the *Fräuleins*. But he is the best in the business, bar none, and he has been with me for more than twenty-five years."

"Pleased to meet you," I said, holding out my hand. But Gehrmann ignored it, turning instead to Offenbach.

"We're busy, Klaus!" he snapped. "Spa is only four days away."

"Please," Offenbach said.

Gehrmann looked from him to me and back to him and finally sighed and nodded. "Very well. What must I do?"

"That's better," Offenbach said, slapping the man on the shoulder. "Show Mr. Carnahan around. Let him see anything he wants to see. But no photographs. And then let him take last year's winner around the oval for a couple of laps."

Offenbach turned to me, a huge grin on his face. "Last year we won at Le Mans. The car was brilliant. I will allow you to drive it to get the feel for our work. That is if you are game?"

That was his surprise. I returned the wide grin. "I'd like nothing better," I said.

Gehrmann was finally smiling, figuring no doubt that I would make a colossal fool of myself with the car. Formula racing machines—and they are machines, not automobiles in the strictest sense of the word—are not the easiest things to drive. The average driver would have no comprehension of what was going on in the cockpit of one of these highly tuned and finely machined beauties. Graduating from an American sedan to one of these cars would be in complexity and driving skill like going from a tricycle to a diesel truck.

The steering on a formula-one machine is touchy, the five-speed transmission stiff and almost unmanageable by ordinary standards, the suspension bone jarring, and the inside of the cockpit incredibly hot. At times during the middle of a summer race, temperatures inside the driver's compartment reach as high as 150 degrees. Drivers often lose as much as eight to ten pounds in sweat during a four-hour race.

And Gehrmann figured I was the patsy who was going to make a fool of myself. But the last laugh was going to be mine, I hoped. I had raced before, more than once. And although I was no expert on the subject, and my shoulder hurt like hell, I can keep up with most of the pack in a race, and I hoped I could do it today.

Offenbach left us, and Gehrmann studied my face again for a moment before he spoke. "Is there anything else in here you would like to see, Herr Carnahan, or would you like to go out to the track immediately? The machine warming up now, as a matter of fact, is the one from last year. We have been testing various new components on the old engine. It is ready for you." He smiled.

"Let's go," I said, and I headed for the doors without waiting for him.

If Gehrmann had been here from the beginning with Offenbach he was probably clean. And if I could put him immediately on the defensive and then impress him with my driving ability, perhaps I could get some answers out of him.

In fifteen minutes I had been suited up with asbestos underwear and socks, a fireproofed jump suit, and light shoes and was pulling the helmet on over my face mask.

The tremendous amount of oil spray and fuel

exhaust in the air when one of these machines was running necessitated the face-mask filter; otherwise, the driver's lungs would become so irritated in such a short time that no man could successfully complete a race.

Gehrmann and another mechanic helped strap me in to the small, tight-fitting cockpit, with aircraft-type over-the-shoulder harnesses.

They pointed out the fire-extinguishing equipment and the gear-shift lever, which was a tiny knob on my right side by my knee, and explained that all the gauges and dials on the instrument panel had been turned so that red line was straight up. If any needle moved farther than the twelve-o'clock position, something was wrong and I should immediately shut down.

"Take it very easy for the first couple of laps," Gehrmann was shouting to me over the roughly idling engine. "Get used to the transmission and brakes and steering. Then take three or four laps to build up your speed and confidence. On the sixth lap I will time you. Don't run more than ten laps."

I gave him thumbs up, eased the car into first gear, and carefully took off from the test apron and entered the highly banked 2.4-mile oval track that was surfaced with rough concrete for good traction.

At the first turn I was going less than fifty miles per hour, still in first gear, and I oversteered so that I came very low on the bank. By the time I had negotiated the turn and started on the back straightaway I was back in the middle of the track, and I punched it. The car seemed almost to shoot out from under me. I popped it in second gear, and it was as if I were shot out of a cannon.

There was no speedometer in the machine, but with the tach readings Gehrmann had thrown at me, I figured I was doing somewhere in the neighborhood of eighty at the second curve, negotiating this one a lot more smoothly.

The steering wheel was very small, and the steering was stiff. But the tiniest movement of the wheel produced an immediate effect, so that curves were made at speed by merely leaning to the left, thus moving the steering wheel slightly. I would be driving literally by the seat of my pants.

Down the home straightaway I shifted into third gear in front of Gehrmann and punched it. It would be now or never, I figured.

Around the first turn of the second lap I was doing better than a hundred, and when I came out of the curve I slammed the car into fourth, jammed the accelerator to the floor, and held on as the engine began to wind up. At the back curve I tapped the brakes, and it was almost as if the car had hit a brick wall, it slowed so fast. I downshifted into third, hit the curve, and shot out of it like a rocket.

Everything now was happening in a blur, and for the time being I forgot about Lisbon, about Hawk, about the president, about Gehrmann, about the crowd of onlookers who had gathered; I concentrated on my driving.

Red line in fourth past Gehrmann; 160 miles per hour; tap the brakes, downshift for the curve, hit the pedal, shift to fourth; red line; shift finally to fifth; back curve approaching 200 miles per hour; downshift to fourth; tap the brakes; downshift to third; back end slides around in a drift. Out of the curve. Shift once, twice. The heat rising.

For a half dozen laps the routine was the same. The machine's feel was coming to me in leaps and bounds, and for a time it was almost as if I were a free spirit, floating and soaring around the two wide curves and the pair of long straightaways. I was welded to the machine. We were a part of each other.

I flashed past Gehrmann at near red line in fifth, two hundred miles per hour plus, and he was waving the red flag, which meant for me to shut down.

At the first curve I hit the brakes and downshifted to fourth around the curve, and then shifted down again to third, and completed the final straightaway at a hundred miles per hour, which seemed almost like a crawling speed to me. Around the last curve and the short straightaway, and I finally pulled off the track onto the apron where Gehrmann stood.

When I shut off the engine, unstrapped, and pulled off my helmet, I could hear the applause.

"Enough!" Gehrmann shouted. "Back to work you sons of bitches. Spa is only four days away."

The crowd dispersed as Gehrmann helped me out of the car and then offered me a drink from his hip flask. I took it and handed it back when I had taken a deep drink of the obviously expensive brandy.

"Not bad," Gehrmann said, "for an amateur. I had you at 207 miles per hour on the last straightaway. A little flashy and fast for this track, perhaps, the corners a little ragged. You never did find the proper slot. But not bad, nevertheless.''

I nodded. ''Now that we know I can drive, I wonder just how well you can drink. Or is that all bluff?''

Gehrmann had paid me a compliment, something rare for him, I figured, and I was returning it with a jibe. He reacted almost as if he had been slapped.

''All right, Carnahan or whatever your name is,'' he snapped. ''I'll see you at six o'clock in the Hansa Haus.''

''I'll find it,'' I said, and Gehrmann stormed off.

XII

"I DON'T LIKE showoffs, I don't like spies, and I especially don't like Communists. Which are you?"

Rudi Gehrmann peered at me through myopic eyes across the small, dirty table in the crowded Hansa Haus bar. I had found the place easily enough, after I had left Offenbach, by merely driving in everwidening circles. I figured whatever bar was Gehrmann's usual hangout would have to be within walking distance from where he worked. I was right. The Hansa Haus was only two blocks away, up a side street in a not-so-nice neighborhood. Perfect for Gehrmann when he took his lunch hours.

This evening the place was crammed with workers from the nearby chemical, plastics, and textile factories, which were less famous than Wiesbaden's hot springs or casino, but nevertheless made up the backbone of this city. No one was paying any attention to us.

We had been sitting here together for about an hour, and already Gehrmann was drunk.

"I don't like spies or Communists either," I replied. "And as far as showing off, I couldn't help myself this afternoon. The machine was too good."

Gehrmann laughed. "You're goddamned right it's good. I built it with my own two hands."

I began my probing gently. "How long have you been with Offenbach?"

Gehrmann almost exploded. "Twenty years, and maybe that's been too long. Too long."

I said nothing, waiting for him to continue. He seemed to be a very troubled man.

"In the beginning it was good. Klaus and me worked together sometimes around the clock. We built good cars in those days. Fine machines. And we won our share of the races together."

I nodded. "And lately?" I prompted.

Gehrmann's eyes seemed to clear of their drunken stupor for a moment. "Who the hell are you, anyway?" he snapped.

"Nick Carnahan, Amalgamated Press."

"Bullshit," Gehrmann bellowed, thumping his fist on the table. No one in the place looked up.

"You tell me, then, who I am," I said calmly.

Gehrmann continued to stare at me, but after a moment he shook his head. "I don't know. You're not from Ferrari, and they're the only competition I'm worried about. And you're not like the others."

"Others?" I said, sitting forward.

"The Communists," he said, waving his hand as if to dismiss the subject.

"What Communists?" I said, pressing him.

"LeMaigne and that Torman woman. Both of them are Communists."

"How do you know that?" I asked.

"Are you with them?" Gehrmann slurred. "Are you one of them?"

I shook my head slowly. "I'm the opposition," I said softly.

Gehrmann reached out and grabbed my arm in his powerful hands. "Stop them before it's too late," he said with feeling. "They're taking over the company. They're taking it away from Klaus, and he can't see it. It was them who got the others to quit. Good men all of them, and they quit two months before Spa. No one wants to work for us now, because we're Communists. Offenbach Motor Works will soon be no more if this keeps up. Stop them."

"You'd better tell me everything you know," I said. "Then maybe I can do something about it."

Gehrmann let go of my arm and poured himself another brandy from the already nearly empty bottle on our table. He had drunk most of it.

He contemplated the contents of the glass,

drank it down, and then lurched to his feet and staggered over to the bar, where he ordered another bottle. When he returned to the table, he opened the bottle, poured himself another drink, and then looked at me.

"LeMaigne was the first," he said. "He's a damned good driver, but he's a bad man. I've tried to tell Klaus about him, but he won't see it. There isn't enough time to worry about such things, he tells me. We've got to be ready by Spa."

"How long ago was that?" I asked.

Gehrmann shrugged. "Six months, maybe nine months, ago we hired LeMaigne. He was a nothing on the circuit until Klaus took him and put him as a team driver alternate. But then after the meetings began and everyone quit, LeMaigne became *the* driver."

This was it. "What meetings?" I asked, leaning forward and lowering my voice.

Gehrmann was drunk now, almost too drunk to make any sense. He stared stupidly at me for several long moments before he answered.

"There were a lot of meetings in the break room late at night. That was when I was still working late. Now I don't bother," he said.

"Who was at these meetings?" I asked urgently, and something of my concern penetrated into his stupor.

"LeMaigne, his girlfriend Inge Torman, and a bunch of others—some of them from the company, but a lot of them strangers. I saw LeMaigne letting those people through the back gate."

"What kind of people? Do you know their names? Descriptions?"

Gehrmann shook his head, and his eyes half-closed. "Arabs, Japanese, Spaniards. I don't know. All kinds of them."

"What did they talk about?" I asked, but Gehrmann was sinking fast. His head nodded, and his eyes closed as he slumped forward on the table.

I pushed him up and held the half-full glass of brandy under his nose. "I need more answers, Gehrmann. What did they talk about at those meetings?"

Gehrmann stared at me but then mumbled something.

"What?" I almost shouted.

"Honolulu," he mumbled. "They talked about Honolulu. And then Tokyo and Cairo and something about Spa."

The Lisbon organization was here after all. And somehow one of the Offenbach employees, probably LeMaigne, was going to pull off the next attempt on the president's life. At Spa, during or just before the race, when the president was in the grandstands.

"Were you at those meetings?" I asked.

Gehrmann shook his head. "I used to hide in the storeroom. You can listen through the ventilating grille to what is happening in the break room."

"Was anyone else from the company in the place at the time?"

"Klaus was sometimes in his office. But the place was usually empty."

"What else did they talk about during those meetings?" I asked. But Gehrmann was too far gone now for any further questioning.

As he sank down on the table again, he whispered something that sounded like "kite." For a moment it did not register on me, but then I put it together. Kite, of course. They were talking about the hang glider that had been used in the Honolulu attempt.

"Did they talk about bombs and hand grenades too?" I asked, lifting Gehrmann's head off the table.

"Bombs . . . hand grenades . . . missiles," he said.

Missiles. The thought struck me dumb. In Honolulu they had used a hang glider. In Tokyo the bombs. And in Cairo the hand grenades. All those things had been spoken of during the meetings that Gehrmann eavesdropped on. And now Spa. And now a missile. They were going to kill the president of the United States with a missile!

I looked down at Gehrmann. He was a good man who could not handle what was happening around him. He had tried to tell Offenbach that something was happening to the company, but Offenbach was too wrapped up in the problem of making it to Spa with three cars to worry about in-plant meetings.

"As long as the work is getting done, I don't care if they hold a dance every night in the break room." I'm sure that's more or less what Offenbach told Gehrmann.

But what kind of missile were they going to use? And exactly when would it be fired? And by whom?

Another connection rammed home with me as well. The red fist tattoo had four fingers on it. One for Honolulu. One for Tokyo. One for Cairo. And evidently one for Spa. Four attempts.

But that must mean they had known all along that the first three attempts were doomed to failure. That didn't make any sense at all.

I pulled Gehrmann's head up by the hair and slapped him across the face. He came to momentarily.

"LeMaigne. Where is he right now?"

"At the plant with the others," Gehrmann mumbled, almost unintelligibly.

"What others?" I asked, but Gehrmann was finally completely out.

I gave the bartender some money to send Gehrmann home in a cab; then I hurried the two blocks to the Offenbach plant, which surprisingly enough, was completely lit up. Several large trucks and a half dozen panel vans were parked in the front of the building, near a set of open garage doors.

As I pulled up and parked across the street, I suddenly remembered that Offenbach had told me they would be moving the cars to Spa sometime this evening. They were evidently getting ready to leave now.

I got out of my rented Mercedes and ambled across the street as several men pushed one of the formula-one Porsches from inside the plant and with the help of a few more men, rolled the car up a set of ramps into the back of one of the trucks.

The car was completely assembled now, including the gleaming, bright white cowling with the Offenbach symbol painted across the top of the spoiler, which looked like a wing above the rear engine.

Offenbach was out front supervising the loading of the machines, tires, spare parts, and tools. When I came up to him he turned to me in surprise and smiled.

"Mr. Carnahan, you've come to see us off?" he boomed.

I pulled him aside. "I came to tell you that your head mechanic, Rudi Gehrmann, is at this moment in a drunken stupor at a bar not far from here."

"The Hansa Haus. I know," he said. "The bartender called me. I sent one of my men over to fetch him. He'll ride to Spa with us in the back of one of the vans, as usual."

Offenbach stared at me for a long moment. "How would you like to quit the news business and come to work for me as a relief driver? I could use another man."

"Not me," I laughed.

"Don't be overmodest, Mr. Carnahan. I watched your performance from my office window this afternoon. In a couple of seasons you could be a serious contender."

"No, thanks," I said. "I just thought I'd stop by to send you off and ask if I could have a word with your head driver."

"LeMaigne?" Offenbach said, scowling.

"Right," I said. "I've spoken with your head mechanic; now I'd like a couple of words with your head driver."

Offenbach shook his head. "I wonder what you must think of us, Mr. Carnahan. My head mechanic is a drunkard, and my head driver you'll learn is not a very pleasant man. The only thing he has going for him, as a matter of fact, is his brilliant driving.''

Offenbach pointed him out to me, down the row of trucks near where the last Porsche was being loaded.

I thanked him and headed that way. LeMaigne may have been the head of the Lisbon organization, but I was sure that if I arrested him now, it would not stop the attempt on the president's life at Spa. Only two things would stop that now. Either the president would have to be convinced not to show up for the race or I would have to find and disarm the missile. If I couldn't do the latter by race time, I was damned well going to make sure the president remained in Frankfurt for the race, with or without his cooperation. Guns, knives, and bombs can be fought, but a missile is practically impossible to stop once it's launched. It's especially unlikely to be stopped by one man armed only with a gas bomb, a stiletto, and a 9-millimeter Luger.

LeMaigne, a dark, narrowed-hipped, but big-shouldered man, stood with his hands behind his back watching as the third Porsche was finally rolled up the ramp into the last truck in the row.

He said something to one of the mechanics, who scurried back into the plant with a helper, and a moment later the two of them emerged with a pair of aluminum loading ramps, which they loaded into the back of the truck with the car. When the rear door of the truck was secured, LeMaigne turned to face me.

"What do you want of me, Mr. Carnahan?" he said precisely, catching me somewhat off-guard.

He noticed the expression on my face. "I caught your unimpressive performance on the track this afternoon. Are you here seeking a job?"

I smiled. LeMaigne was smooth. No doubt there were several people now working for Offenbach who were reporting directly to LeMaigne. It would have to work that way if the Lisbon organization was to have any security whatsoever. I only wondered whether LeMaigne had connected me with the presidential party, or if he was taking me for what I appeared to be, a newsman with the Amalgamated Press.

"No job," I said. "I merely wanted to ask you how a mutual friend of ours is doing these days."

LeMaigne's eyes narrowed, but he said nothing, waiting for me to continue. The final act of the Lisbon organization, set to unfold at Spa, was already in motion. Everyone except LeMaigne— at least everyone important—was now underground and would probably not surface until just before the attempt was to be made. I could not allow things to progress that far, however. I was going to have to find the missile. The only way I could do that was to make them nervous, cause them to get sloppy and make a mistake.

"I'm talking about Inge Torman," I said carefully, but there was absolutely no reaction, other than a slight irritation, in LeMaigne's expression.

"Torman?" he said. "I don't believe I've heard the name."

"That's odd," I said. "I spoke with her not more

than two months ago, and she mentioned your name."

I did not wait for him to answer; instead, I turned and started to leave. But then I stopped and turned back momentarily. "By the way, good luck with everything at Spa."

XIII

AFTER I LEFT LeMaigne, I wished Offenbach good luck and assured him that I would be at Spa for the race. As I drove away, I could see LeMaigne in my rear-view mirror, watching me leave. Then I turned the corner.

Instead of heading toward Frankfurt to await the president, I went around the block so that I was on one of the side streets that intersected with Max Schiller Strasse. I got out of the car and walked the few feet to the corner and peered around the building.

Offenbach and his crew and all the vehicles were still parked half a block from me, but at first I could not pick out LeMaigne.

He had been standing at the rear of the last truck, but now he was nowhere in sight. For a moment I thought he might have already left, but then I saw him hurry out of the plant and approach Offenbach, and the two of them began talking and gesturing. I was sure that LeMaigne had come up with some excuse why he could not leave with the rest of the crew this evening. And Offenbach was not buying it.

It was almost eight o'clock and dark in this section of the city, although to the west, toward the center of town, the sky was brightly lit. The streets would be full of people now, shopping, going out for dinner, making ready to go up the hill to the casino. Wiesbaden was a very classy town. At least, most of it was.

LeMaigne finally broke away from Offenbach and hurried back into the plant. A few minutes later he drove out in a small, yellow Fiat Spyder sports car and headed my way.

Quickly I ran back to my rented Mercedes, jumped in, and started the engine but did not turn on the lights.

LeMaigne flashed by the side street where I was parked, and headed back toward the center of town. He had taken my bait, and whoever he was going to see now would have to be someone very important in the Lisbon organization—if Gehrmann had been telling me the truth.

I pulled around the corner and headed down

Max Schiller Strasse away from the Offenbach plant, in the direction LeMaigne had gone. Several blocks away I could see the taillights on his car, and I sped up to close up the gap. I did not want to lose him.

There was a possibility, I had to admit to myself, that Gehrmann was nothing more than a drunk who harbored resentment at the changes that Offenbach had made recently. Perhaps he was jealous of LeMaigne for some reason, in which case I was on a wild-goose chase. Perhaps LeMaigne was nothing more than he appeared to be—a damned good driver with a lousy disposition. In that case, I was wasting valuable time.

But something inside me told me that was not true. Otherwise, why had he apparently taken my bait? Why had he left within a few minutes after I had mentioned the name Inge Torman?

I had originally planned to follow LeMaigne all the way to Spa, if need be. I was hoping he would attempt to contact someone there. But I had not expected he would bolt so quickly. Evidently I had upset him enough for him to telephone someone as soon as I left him, make his excuses to Offenbach, and now head to a meeting somewhere.

A few minutes later LeMaigne pulled up a side street, and a few blocks later, he parked across the avenue from a small café just off the Wilhelmstrasse, Wiesbaden's most elegant street of shops, restaurants, and clubs.

I quickly pulled into a narrow hotel parking lot a few doors from the café, paid the surprised attendant, and then followed LeMaigne on foot.

The man was just crossing the avenue, and at first I thought he would enter the café, but he did not. Instead, he strolled past the front door of the establishment and continued down the street, as if he was out for a leisurely evening stroll.

I followed about half a block back.

Traffic was light and there were few people out walking along this narrow side street, but when LeMaigne turned on to the Wilhelmstrasse it was as if we had gone suddenly from a quiet country village at night to the main thoroughfare of the busy city in broad daylight.

Neon signs, bright street lights, and even a pair of huge searchlights in front of one newly opened club lit up the wide avenue and crowded sidewalks like daytime. Couples dressed in evening clothes strolled along the broad sidewalks, talking and laughing, and the street was crowded with traffic.

For a few minutes I lost LeMaigne in the crowds, but then I suddenly saw him dart across the street through the heavy traffic. A moment later he had switched directions on me and was walking the way he had come, but on the opposite side of the street and now arm in arm with a tall, redhaired woman.

For the next half hour I was kept busy dodging pedestrians as I tried to keep up with LeMaigne and the woman. She seemed vaguely familiar to me somehow, even at this distance.

Finally I was able to make it across the street in a break in traffic, and I managed to come within a few yards of them, not close enough to hear what they were saying, but definitely close enough to see who the woman was.

I wasn't surprised in the least to realize that the redhaired woman was the same one who had shot and killed Maria Oeriés in Lisbon. I had only caught a brief glimpse of her then through the crack in the door, but I was certain the woman now with LeMaigne was the same one.

And now any reservations or slight doubts I had entertained, about what Gehrmann had told me, evaporated.

The redhaired woman was Inge Torman. She and LeMaigne were at least members of the Lisbon organization, if not its leaders. And I was sure they were key elements in the last planned attempt on the president's life, set for Sunday at Spa.

Still, there was the matter of the missile—finding it, disarming it, and finding out who would actually trigger it. Until I had that information, the president would not be safe. I was certain that as well organized as the Lisbon group was, they would not allow any attempt to be totally dependent upon one or two people. I was sure that if I stopped LeMaigne and the Torman woman, the attempt on Magnesen's life would continue on schedule.

And that was only half of my assignment. I still had to learn why the organization wanted President Magnesen dead and how the organization had come up with the president's itinerary.

There were dozens of other questions plaguing me as well. Such as: Olanda Williamson. How did she fit into all this? Stanley Magnesen. Was he an unwitting part of this plot, with his talk against his father's world tour for peace?

How about the assassins themselves? Once before I had run into a group of fanatics all willing to give their lives in an attempt to terrorize society. The had all been Japanese. They had all believed in the *kamikaze* spirit of World War II. But what of these people?

Portenjo gave his life in Honolulu for an attempt on the president's. The two young Japanese terrorists in Tokyo and the Arab in Cairo had known they would not come out of it alive. What was their motivation?

The two I was following walked for several blocks along the Wilhelmstrasse, apparently two lovers out for an evening stroll. They stopped from time to time to look in shop windows and talk, and then they would continue as if they didn't have a care in the world.

Finally they turned off down a back street, and the moment they were out of sight I rushed to catch up. I did not want them slipping down an alleyway or into a building before I caught up to them.

I eased my way carefully around the corner in time to see them running toward a parked van. They knew they were being followed. How? And where were they going?

Alarm bells jangling once again along my nerves, I headed in a dead run after them, and as I ran I loosened my jacket and withdrew my Luger. As I was about to pull the safety catch off, I sensed someone standing in a darkened doorway to my right. I was about to swivel around, when I saw the club coming toward my head, and even in that split second I knew I was too late. And then it was as if a bomb had been set off in my head, and I could see the sidewalk rushing up to meet my face.

I don't know how many times I've been bashed over the head, but each time it seems to get a little more unpleasant. Each time it seems as if a little part of me has been left behind on the club. This moment was no exception.

Consciousness came back to me in nauseating waves, as I blinked to focus my eyes on the cold pavement in front of my nose.

LeMaigne and Inge Torman. I had been running after them when someone hit me on the head. They had been waiting for me. They had maneuvered me down that back street.

In Lisbon, with the elevator, the Torman woman had outsmarted me, and now here in Wiesbaden she had done it again.

I tried to move my arms, which felt as if they were being slowly stretched out of their sockets, and realized that I had been tied up. The rope had been looped around my arms and then pulled tight around my ankles, bowing my entire body backward. My head hurt. The stitches where the shrapnel had been taken out of my shoulder had pulled loose, and I could feel I was bleeding. I was so nauseated and dizzy that I was sure I would vomit at any moment.

By degrees, I became aware of other things around me as well. First I could smell water, or more accurately, the waterfront. Probably the

Rhein. I had been knocked unconscious, tied up, and taken down to the warehouse district.

I managed to swivel my head around a few inches so that I could look up. Inge Torman stood a few feet from me, talking with two men, obviously dock workers by their dress and looks. They were too far away for me to hear what they were saying, but it seemed they were arguing. The Torman woman was gesturing with her hands back the way my feet were pointed.

When they noticed that I had regained consciousness, Inge Torman broke away from them, came over to me, and squatted down by my side.

"Sunday your president will be dead," she said to me, almost conversationally. Her voice was soft, with a slight German accent. I was sure that she had been born German but had been raised, or at least educated, in the United States. Probably on the East Coast.

"Why?" I managed to croak. My mouth and throat were dry, and the effort to speak seemed almost impossible.

The woman smiled wryly. "It is an exercise, Mr. Carter, nothing more."

This was making less and less sense the further we went. She must have caught my confusion from my expression, because she reached out and gently touched my cheek.

"I imagine this has all been very confusing to you. Honolulu. Tokyo, Cairo. All those attempts were meant to fail. You worked out very nicely for us."

"But Spa won't fail," I said.

She shook her head and slowly stood up. "No, Spa will not fail. Nor will any of this fail to show the world just how vulnerable the president of the United States—or any government leader, for that matter—is. Perhaps the next leader your country elects will be a more sane, responsive person."

I struggled to sit up, but the woman almost nonchalantly nudged my sore shoulder with the toe of her shoe and I fell back to the pavement, the pain exploding along my side and down my back.

She crouched down next to me again. "You will be dead in a few minutes, so I suppose it will not hurt to clear up this mystery for you."

I looked frantically around me. LeMaigne was nowhere in sight, and the two men who had been talking with Inge Torman were leaning up against a rough brick building about twenty feet away, smoking and staring past us at the river.

The place we were at was very dark. A lone light atop a building about a block away was the only illumination nearby.

The woman had taken a snub-nosed .38 revolver out of her purse, and she screwed a silencer onto the end of its threaded barrel. The silencer was longer than the gun.

"Our organization did not begin in Lisbon, as you have suspected all along," the woman began.

"The radio message . . . "

"It was a decoy, meant only to excite your curiosity. We wanted you to come after us, to try to stop us. We wanted you to see how futile it is."

I wanted to stall for time. I was about to speak, when the thought struck me: Stall for time for what purpose? There was no way I was going to get loose from the ropes that held me. The cavalry wasn't coming. No one knew where I was. The only contact I had had with my office was the óne call Offenbach had made to our blind number in Frankfurt.

But I could not give up. For an instant a picture of the young Amalgamated Press office manager in Honolulu flashed in my mind. He had wanted to be a Killmaster, but I had known he would never make it because he did not have the overdeveloped instinct for survival that I had. And now I was giving up.

I began to work my wrists back and forth against the ropes. "You'll never get away with it," I said, mustering up what strength and resolve I had to make my voice clear and put a smile on my lips.

The woman laughed lightly. "Why not?"

"Because your plan is known. We know about the missile at Spa. We know when the attempt will be made. We know about LeMaigne. About the meetings at Offenbach. We know about it all."

For an instant a flash of concern crossed her face, but then it was replaced by the same almost innocent smile. "Missile, you say?" she mocked me. "*We* know," she said, emphasizing the first word. "It won't work. Your people may know that you are in Wiesbaden. They also know that you were at the Offenbach plant. But that's all. If they come here looking for you, they'll find Offenbach and the crew gone. Nothing more."

"How do you know that?" I snapped.

"Very easy—" she started, when suddenly the

top of her head disappeared backward in a spray of blood and white, pulverized bone. An instant later I heard the roar of a heavy-caliber hand gun, probably a .357 or .44 magnum.

The woman's body flipped backward, and her legs jerked violently against my chest and face as her body went through its death throes.

Two other shots rang out in the night, and I was able to look up in time to see both men who had been with the woman pitch forward.

The cavalry had arrived.

For several long minutes everything was deathly still, the quiet even more obvious after the gunfire. Inge Torman's body had stopped its spasmodic twitchings. I suddenly became aware that someone was standing behind me.

I managed to swivel my entire body painfully around to look up into the face of Derrick Stone, holding a Reuger .357 magnum revolver in his hand. For an instant there was a strange look on the man's face, in his eyes; then he grinned.

"Looks like I made it just in time," he said, and he holstered his gun, bent down, and began untying me.

"How in the hell did you manage that?" I asked. Something was wrong here, drastically wrong.

"The president got word in Moscow that you were here in Wiesbaden at the Offenbach Motor Works," he said, undoing the knots around my ankles. "He told me that you were investigating the assassination plot and figured that since you hadn't checked in, you might be in trouble. So he sent me."

"From Moscow this fast?" I asked as the ropes came loose around my wrists and he helped me to my feet.

Stone laughed. "The president explained it all to Brezhnev, if you can believe that. The Russians put me on one of their jet fighter-interceptors and flew me in to East Berlin. From there I was driven across to the West zone, where I hopped a ride to Frankfurt aboard one of our own jets."

"How did you know where to find me?"

"Pure blind luck," Stone said. "I showed up at the Offenbach plant about the time you took off after the Fiat."

"So you followed me?"

Stone nodded. "I wanted to see where this was leading; otherwise I would have stopped this when they knocked you on the head."

"What about LeMaigne?" I asked. "What happened to him?"

"You mean the man who was with this woman?" Stone said, looking down at the nearly decapitated body of Inge Torman.

I nodded.

"After they loaded you in the van, they dropped the man back at his Fiat, and he took off. I had the choice of following either him or you. I chose you."

The effects of the shrapnel wound and the blow on my head were even more painfully obvious to me now that I was on my feet. As my knees began to buckle, I reached out for Stone, who helped me up.

"The president will be in Frankfurt tomorrow

morning. Meanwhile, I think I'd better get you to a doctor."

My mind was whirling, and it seemed as if someone were drilling down through the top of my skull with a rusty bit. I knew that I had all the information I needed now to figure this thing out. Inge Torman, before she died, had given me almost everything I needed to know. But instead of making any sense, everything was a jumbled mess in my mind.

As I slid into unconsciousness once again, I clung to the one idea that if I could not find the missile in Spa by race time on Sunday, I would have to convince the president to return to Washington.

For once in my career I had run into an organization that was stronger than me—perhaps even smarter than me. They had outwitted me, outmaneuvered me, and outrun me the entire distance. It was as if they had been toying with me all along. Whoever was heading this plot had to be a brilliant person—brilliant but twisted.

XIV

"YOU HAVE A severe concussion. If you leave this hospital you'll probably be dead within the hour."

I was standing next to my bed pulling on my shirt as the nurse who had discovered me up was patiently trying to explain to me why I should get back into bed. Under any other circumstances I would have obliged her; she was quite good-looking and obviously concerned about me beyond her professional capacity.

But remaining in bed even another minute was totally impossible.

I had awakened about a half an hour ago, rang for the nurse, and asked her for the time. It was dark outside, and I was sure it was early Saturday morning. The last thing I remembered was fainting against Stone on the waterfront in Wiesbaden.

"Never mind the time," she had snapped at me.

"What time is it?" I insisted, sitting up, my head whirling around a gigantic split in my skull that had to be the size of the Grand Canyon.

"Two in the morning," she finally said in exasperation.

I lay back in bed. "I want out of here first thing in the morning," I told her. I desperately needed the sleep. Every muscle in my body was screaming for it.

"Impossible," she told me. "We wouldn't discharge you on a Sunday even if you were in any condition to get up. Now get to sleep or I'll give you a sedative to make you sleep."

My mind was whirling in circles. I was seeing LeMaigne and Offenbach arguing. And then I was seeing Inge Torman, the back of her head blowing away in slow motion.

How long I lay like that in a half stupor, I don't know, but suddenly what the nurse had told me began to sink in. "Wouldn't discharge you on a Sunday," the nurse had said.

I sat up in the darkened room. Sunday. I had been unconscious from Friday night, when Stone had rescued me, all Saturday and Saturday night, and now it was Sunday morning—race day!

My clothes were pressed and neatly hung in the closet, and my weapons, all of them, were in the bedside table. For a moment I had to smile. I'm sure that whoever undressed me had found my choice of weapons unusual, especially Pierre, the gas bomb.

The door had opened, and the light had come on as I was finishing dressing. It was the same nurse, and now she was threatening to call the orderlies.

I looked up at her, narrowed my eyes, and mustered as much firmness in my voice as I could. "Fräulein," I said, "if anyone tries to stop me I will hurt them."

My statement was simple, but I think she believed me, because she backed away a few feet. "I'll call the police," she said.

I smiled at her as I finished buttoning my shirt and painfully pulled my holster over my sore shoulder. The motion caused me to wince involuntarily with the pain, and the nurse rushed to my side to help me.

"Insanity," she muttered in German. "Pure insanity. You are going to kill yourself, and I will be to blame."

As I said, the young woman was good-looking, unlike some nurses who have attended me, and it seemed the natural thing to take her into my arms and kiss her. When we parted she seemed out of breath.

"I must go," I told her gently, "but I will tell them it was not your fault."

"Your president called here personally about you," she said, not moving away from me. Her body felt soft and warm, and I almost wished the situation were different.

"That's why I must go," I said, and I disengaged her arms from me.

She helped me with my coat after I had strapped my stiletto, in its specially designed chamois case, to my right forearm. But when I tried to undo the bandage wrapped around my head like a turban, she stopped me.

"What are you doing?" she cried in horror.

"I can't go out like this," I said, brushing her away. A moment later the bandage was off. I explored the large lump on the back of my head, and I could feel the stitches. There must have been at least a dozen.

The nurse was correct about one thing, I thought. I probably wouldn't get very far in my condition. For a moment standing there I was seeing double, and then for a few seconds the room went dim, until I was able to refocus my eyes. But I could not stay here—not when the president was going to Spa in a few hours. He would have to be warned.

I kissed the nurse one last time and then brushed past her and left the hospital, no one on the night shift even noticing me.

Not until I was out in the chill night air, and had walked three blocks before I found a taxi, did something about the hospital strike me as odd. There had been no guard on my room.

It's not that I'm used to having guards on my room every time I get hurt, but this time I would have thought Stone would have ordered a guard on me after the attempt to kill me.

"The Hotel Intercontinental," I told the cabbie.

I sat back in my seat and closed my eyes.

It was just three o'clock in the morning. The race began at one this afternoon, just ten hours from now. In ten hours I was going to have to have this thing solved. Not only was I going to have to stop one more attempt on Magnesen's life, but I was also going to have to find out who besides LeMaigne was behind the plot, as well as answer the one question I was not even close to answering at this moment: Why? Why kill the president of the United States? I mean, why besides the obvious reasons of fanatic terrorism. I was sure there was some reason beyond that—some very specific reason.

Inge Torman had told me that the first three attempts had been nothing more than an exercise. An exercise in what? And for what? What twisted mind would perceive of the assassination of a president as an exercise?

There were a number of other questions still hammering inside my head, in time with the throbbing pain that beat in wave after wave through my body.

Olanda Williamson. I still had not figured where she fit in all this, if indeed she did fit. Perhaps she was nothing more than what she appeared to be, a beautiful but spoiled writer for an intellectual magazine trying for the scoop on the first family.

What about Stanley Magnesen? I was getting my fill of spoiled children on this assignment, and I was liking it less and less as time went on. What had Stanley wanted to talk to me about in Tokyo that he suddenly found he could not say? Was it anything of importance?

And what about the president himself? Magnesen had been acting strange on and off ever since we had left Honolulu for Tokyo. One minute he wanted this case solved; the next, he wanted me back in Washington and the investigation stopped. One minute he was charging full steam ahead on his world tour—damn the assassination attempts—and the next, he was balking, ready to return to Washington, to give it all up. Did the president know something that was affecting his decision-making capabilities? If so, what was it?

Last, there was Derrick Stone—presidential bodyguard, Medal of Honor winner, a highly intelligent but strange man. His appearance in Wiesbaden was nothing short of miraculous. Or was it?

The cabbie broke me out of my reverie, and I opened my eyes and looked up. We were there.

I paid the driver and entered the lobby of the hotel. A pair of Secret Service guards were standing duty at one of the elevators, and when I approached them their eyes went wide.

"It's not polite to stare," I said, smiling. I recognized both of them. The taller man had been a close friend of the Secret Service agent who had died protecting the president in Tokyo. The other usually worked as an installation guard.

"Mr. Stone said you were in the hospital," the one said. "In critical condition."

"They made a mistake," I said. *But not by very much,* I thought.

"Welcome back," the other agent said.

"I've got to get upstairs to see the president," I said softly.

"No can do," one of them said. "Mr. Stone left strict orders that the Man was not to be disturbed. He's leaving for Spa at ten."

Suddenly a connection was made in my mind, and the fuzz seemed to lift for a moment as some of the pieces started to fall into place. "Then I must see him," I insisted.

Both men started to protest, but I cut them off and lowered my voice conspiratorially. "There will be another attempt at Spa. I must tell the president."

"Christ," the one swore. He looked at his partner, who shrugged, and then they stepped aside and punched the elevator button. "He's probably asleep. Shall we call Mr. Stone?"

"Don't bother," I said, as the elevator doors opened and I stepped inside. "I'll take my chances."

"Yes, sir," they said, and the elevator doors closed and the car started up.

The routine was much the same on the top floor, and in addition I had to give up my Luger to the two agents, who seemed genuinely pleased to see me on my feet and back on the job. But they, too, warned me that the president was asleep and that Stone had left strict orders not to disturb him.

The president's appointments secretary, however, was a different matter. The man was definitely not pleased to see me, and he told me so in no uncertain terms.

"I don't want you here at this hour, Mr. Carter," the man sniffed indignantly. "The president desperately needs his rest, and if I may say so, you look as if you belong in a hospital."

"Can't wait, my good man," I said, mocking his slightly effeminate accent. "I must see the president immediately. And if you won't let me through, I'll go past you."

The man stiffened and then stood up straight to his full, unimpressive five feet six. I was certain the man was ready and willing to fight me. Not a bad sort to have on your side. I could not be mean to him.

"Look," I said, again putting a conspiratorial tone in my voice, "there will be another attempt on his life at Spa. Do you want the president to go to the race not knowing that?"

The man seemed to waver, and finally his defenses crumbled. "I'm sorry, Mr. Carter, but everything has been in a terrible state around here since Cairo. The younger Mr. Magnesen is not speaking with his father. That Williamson woman is hanging on everyone. And Mr. Stone has been browbeating the president about his duties. I don't know what to do."

I reached out and patted the man on the arm. "I'll take care of it," I said. "I have so far, haven't I?"

"Yes, sir," the man said. "You seem to be the only one around here who can make the president understand."

I followed the prim but very dedicated little man into the president's sitting room, where he indicated a seat for me and told me he would awaken the president. And then he was gone from the room.

I sank down into the plush, deeply cushioned easy chair, laid my head back, and closed my eyes.

AXE has a rest-and-recuperation ranch in Arizona for its people who have been battered on assignments. I had been there many times, and I would be going there after this thing was completed. But for one of the rare times in my career, I was beginning to wonder seriously if I was going to make it that far this time.

Once again the feeling that I had been outmaneuvered and outsmarted washed through my body like paint thinner on a freshly painted surface. It seemed to wash away all my resolve and what little strength I possessed. I was beginning to wonder if I would last.

"You look like hell," the president said, coming into the room.

I opened my eyes and slowly sat up. "I feel like hell too, Mr. President," I said.

Magnesen sat down in a chair a few feet from mine and stared at me. "When Stone told me what happened in Wiesbaden, I called David Hawk."

The cobwebs suddenly cleared from my mind, and I held my breath. If Hawk ordered me off this assignment finally, it was going to be one order I was going to disobey.

"But he told me something I already knew," the president continued. "That you are a good man, that you would probably disobey any orders calling you off this assignment, so I might just as well go along with you.''

I breathed a sigh of relief.

''There will be another attempt on my life at Spa, is that what you've come here to tell me?'' the president asked, and I could hear the weariness and a note of worry in his voice.

''Yes, sir,'' I said tiredly. ''But before I tell you what I have found out, I need the answers to a couple of questions.''

The president stared at me for several long seconds before he nodded. ''If I can.''

''You must, sir,'' I said. ''First.''

The president seemed to hold his breath waiting for my question.

''Who did the background check on Olanda Williamson before she was allowed to join you and your son on this trip?''

The president seemed surprised by this question, and he had to think a moment. ''I don't know,'' he said. ''I assume it was Derrick Stone personally. He usually handles such matters.''

''Second question.'' I said, and again the president seemed to be holding his breath.

''Do you think your son has had something to do with this plot?''

''My God!'' the president said, half-rising from his chair.

I did not flinch a muscle, and just as fast as the president had risen from his chair in reaction, he seemed to deflate like a toy balloon that has been popped. He slumped back in his chair and buried his face in his hands. "Yes," he said. "God help me . . . yes."

"It's not true, Mr. President," I said, with more conviction in my voice than I had in my mind.

The president looked up at me. "You're sure?"

"Yes sir," I said. "But would you mind explaining why you thought so?" With Magnesen believing that of his son, it explained why he vacillated about my being on this case. If his son was a part of the plot, a portion of the president's heart did not want it discovered.

The president hesitated a moment, trying to pick his words. "His actions and his words. He has been against my trip from the beginning. His friends all are radicals at the university. And each time they tried—in Honolulu, Tokyo, and then Cairo, where he stayed behind in the car—he was nowhere near the assassination attempt."

"Circumstantial," I said.

"Do you know who is behind this?" he said. "Did you find out something in Wiesbaden?"

"Yes to both questions," I said. "But I'm going to need your help not only to stop them, but to prove it. Are you willing?"

"Anything," the president said. "I'll do anything at all."

It was nearly six o'clock in the morning by the time I finally left the president and made it to the room in the luxurious hotel that had been assigned to me one floor below.

I was deeply tired, more tired I think than I have ever been in my life, but there was one more thing to accomplish before I would be able to get any sleep.

I lay down on my bed, my jacket off and my stiletto in my right hand, and waited. The lights were out, the bed was soft, and I had to fight sleep, reviewing over and over again the things I had told the president.

I had drawn a number of conclusions from what Inge Torman had told me in Wiesbaden before Stone killed her, as well as what the president had inadvertently told me. And now I was fairly certain I knew who was behind this plot, but still I did not know why—or exactly how and when the missile would be used against the president at Spa.

I hoped that this morning I would get the answers to at least one of those questions.

A half hour later my door, which I had purposely left unlocked, silently swung open, and Olanda Williamson, dressed only in a nightgown, her body outlined by the light in the corridor, slipped inside and closed the door behind her.

For the brief moment I had got a clear look at her, I had seen she was holding something tightly against her bosom.

In the darkness I silently moved to the far side of the bed and waited for her to come to me. And come to me she did.

I felt the wind from her arm as something struck the bed a few inches from me. I reached out and grabbed her arm, and she exploded into a ball of raging fury, battering at my head with her free hand, something raking against my chest like a hot awl.

For what seemed like an eternity, I struggled with the woman, who seemed half-insane. But it was a strange fight. Neither of us uttered a sound other than our low grunts and soft moans.

Olanda, who had been a part of this all along, did not want to raise the alarm and have the guards stop her from killing me. And I did not want to raise the alarm, but with a different purpose in mind.

For one frightening moment I thought she was going to win. In my weakened condition, with Olanda battering at my head and wounded shoulder, I was beginning to black out; but suddenly, my right hand touched her throat. In the next instant I let go of her arm, and with both hands, mustering up what little strength I had remaining, I sharply twisted her neck backward.

When her neck broke, the noise was a sickeningly soft crunch, and she went suddenly and finally limp in my arms.

A moment later I passed out on the bed.

XV

I REGAINED CONSCIOUSNESS around nine o'clock in the morning and forced myself to get out of the bed. Olanda Williamson, who had been beautiful in life, was a grisly sight in death. Her body was sprawled across my bed, her head at an unnatural angle, her mouth set in a mad grimace, and her eyes wide open, staring at nothing. In her right hand she held a deadly-looking, ornately jeweled dagger with which she had meant to murder me. But under whose orders?

I stood at the edge of the bed looking down at her. Portenjo had died in Honolulu, the two Japanese terrorists in Tokyo, the other man and then Maria Oeriés in Lisbon, the Arab outside Cairo, Inge Torman and her two friends in Wiesbaden, and now Olanda Williamson in Frankfurt.

The Lisbon organization had left a trail of death behind it. How many more people would die this day before it was all over?

And still I had none of the answers. I had hoped that whoever would come for me this morning would make a mistake, so that I could subdue them alive. I had hoped that I could get a few answers. But now I had nothing, or almost nothing.

Every muscle and nerve in my body screamed for rest as I managed to drag Olanda's body off the bed and stuff it into a closet. It would be discovered as soon as the maids entered the room to clean later this morning, but by then I would be in Spa and the last chapter of this grisly business would be unfolding.

I spent a long time in the shower, first letting the exceedingly hot water beat against my protesting body, and then letting the cold spray revive me somewhat.

After I was dressed, I oiled my Luger and checked its action, sharpened my stiletto, and selected a longer-range, more deadly gas bomb for my thigh pouch.

This was the end of it. Either the conclusions I had drawn were correct and I would have a chance of winning, or they were completely wrong and I would probably lose. Either way, the next few hours would determine the outcome.

I left my room and went upstairs. I was let into the president's suite by his appointments secretary. The president, dressed and ready to go, was talking with his son Stanley and Derrick Stone. They all looked up when I entered the room.

"Good morning, Nick," the president said jovially. "Care for some coffee before we leave?"

I smiled and nodded. "Love some," I said, mustering as much lightness in my voice as I could.

Stanley had jumped up from where he was sitting. He was looking at me as if he were seeing a ghost. Stone remained seated, but his mouth had dropped open.

Stanley was the first to speak. "I thought you were . . . ."

"In the hospital?" I finished for him. "I was, but they released me."

"I would have thought you'd be in the hospital for quite a while," Stone said, finding his voice at last.

The president's secretary brought me my coffee, and I sat down on the edge of the couch at just the moment my knees would have given out.

I looked directly at Stone. "I wouldn't miss Spa for the world," I said, sipping my coffee.

Stanley had looked from me to Stone and then to his father, an almost wild expression on his face. When he spoke his voice was cracking. "There's going to be another attempted assassination at Spa, isn't there?" he said to his father. "They're going to try to kill you again."

President Magnesen shrugged.

"No!" Stanley wailed. "No . . . I'm not going. This is nuts." He jumped up. "This entire goddamned tour has been crazy. It's been crazy since the beginning. And now you're going to the stupid race and let them take another potshot at you? Sooner or later they're going to win. I'm just not going. Olanda and I are returning to the States. Now. This morning."

He stormed out of the room, and another piece of the puzzle fell into place for me. When I had told the president earlier that Stanley was not a part of the Lisbon organization, I had been guessing. Now I knew it was true. The only reason Stanley was never around when his father was in public was because he was a coward. After the attempt on the president's life in Honolulu, Stanley kept out of the way.

I only wished I could explain to him about Olanda. He was going to do some frantic searching this morning for her, and when her body was finally discovered in my room, he was going to be a miserable, confused young man. It was something his own father was going to have to sort out for him when this was all over.

The president's secretary entered the room. "Your helicopter is ready, Mr. President," he announced, and we all stood.

"To Spa," I said, raising my cup in toast. I took another sip of the coffee and then put the cup down. *To Spa,* I said to myself, *if I can make it that long*.

Spa from the air is a pleasing little town. It is a commune of ten thousand persons in Belgium's province Liège just across the border from Germany and only a little more than a hundred air miles from Frankfurt.

More than two hundred thousand people had gathered for the Grand Prix race, which each year brought fame to the area and fortune to its merchants.

Four helicopters, loaned to the presidential party, had left the Frankfurt airport at 11:00 A.M. sharp, and now, shortly after noon, we were hovering over a flat area behind the grandstands.

The racetrack is nothing more than three intersecting highways that, once each year, are blocked off to make up the roughly oval course. Filled with curves, switchbacks, hills, and a few long straightaways, the circuit at Spa is considered, nevertheless, one of the easier courses, unlike Monaco, which is run through city streets, or Nuremberg Ring, with its terrible negative-banked curves.

The course is a couple of miles outside Spa, and we could see the long lines of cars, campsites, and parking lots that stretched the entire distance.

The president, Stone, two other Secret Service agents, and I were in the first helicopter, along with a couple of German officials. The other machines carried other Secret Service agents and several Belgium officials who had met us in Frankfurt to facilitate our entry without customs checks into Belgium.

We came down a hundred feet from a knot of at least two hundred people, most of them, I guessed, journalists from all over the world, as well as local and federal Belgian officials.

The president leaned over toward me as we touched down. "Are you up to this, Carter?" he said over the noise of the helicopter's blades.

"Yes, sir," I said, nodding. But I seriously wondered whether I was.

Stone had noticed the exchange, and he leaned toward us. "Anything the matter, sir?" he said.

The president shook his head. "This will be an interesting race," he said.

The mayor of Spa, the director of the International Racing Federation, and the federal official from Brussels, whose exact title I never did get greeted the president when he stepped down from the helicopter.

Stone's men formed a cordon around the little group, fending off the newspeople and leading the group to the rear entrance of the large grandstand on a slight hill. To the left the track made its famous switchback about a quarter of a mile away. A restaurant was on the far side of the track, at the curve, which was actually one of the highway intersections.

The straightaway that led down the hill past the grandstand curved up and to the right about a half mile farther, and then the track was lost to the trees up the hill.

When the president and his party were settled in their box seats, a light lunch with wine was served them, while Stone followed me down to trackside

People and cars were everywhere on the track and in the pits. I looked at my watch as we stepped down onto the concrete surface. It was shortly before twelve-thirty. In a little more than a half hour the race would begin.

I turned and looked back up to where the president was seated. There were at least thirty Secret Service agents in his immediate vicinity, and scanning the crowd, I knew that there were another fifty scattered here and there.

But a hundred times that number would do absolutely no good against a missile.

Stone spoke, and it was as if he had been reading my mind. "If we had a thousand men on him today it wouldn't be enough," he said.

I looked at him. "Then it's up to us."

Stone nodded. "I tried to convince him this morning to cancel out, but he insisted. There was nothing I could do."

As we had entered the grandstands from the rear, I had noticed the three big Offenbach trucks parked, and now I looked toward the Offenbach pit less than twenty yards away. Offenbach was there, along with a dozen other people, but LeMaigne was nowhere in sight. I was certain that he was there, however, or nearby.

Stone was watching me when I turned back to him. "Any ideas where we begin?" I asked.

"Offenbach," Stone said. "I noticed their trucks out back. Why don't we snoop around and see what's back there?"

"All right," I said.

We worked our way through the crowd and behind the grandstands, headed for the three Offenbach trucks that were parked among several dozen other similar race-machine transporters. Stone was a few feet behind me and to my left as we hurried across the soft ground toward the graveled area where the trucks were parked.

No one was near the Offenbach trucks, and the back doors were unlocked. I opened the first one and peered inside. Along the inside walls were tool racks and spare-parts bins, and near the front of the truck were several large packing crates, any one of which could have held a missile large enough to do the job.

I jumped inside, Stone directly behind me, and worked my way to the forward section of the huge trailer. As I got to the front, the trailer's rear door closed and all the light was cut off, plunging us into absolute darkness.

Silently I crouched down and scooted to my left as something metallic clanged against the forward wall where I had been standing a moment before. And then there was silence.

I half-crouched and half-lay against what felt like an engine block, my stiletto in hand, waiting for Stone to make the next move. This had not come as a complete surprise to me, although I was disappointed.

Stone had evidently been the man behind this from the very beginning. He was the only one I had met who had the brains and the military-operations knowledge to make such an organization work. He was the one who knew the president's every move, which he piped back to his people. It had been him all along. But why?

"How did you figure me out?" Stone's voice came from the rear of the trailer.

I edged behind the engine block and lay as flat to

the floor as possible, using the massive hunk of steel as a shield.

"It had to be either you, Olanda, or Stanley. You were the only ones who had the president's itinerary, or access to it, and yet the brains to pull something like this off."

"Why not Stanley?" Stone said, laughing. He had not moved yet.

"He's a coward," I said. "Besides, the president is his father. And no matter how much his son disagrees with him, you can still see they are father and son."

"Very good. And Olanda?"

"I figured Olanda was too good to be true and was probably in on this, but she wasn't bright enough to organize it, I learned. Someone else had to do that."

"The process of elimination," Stone said. "My compliments."

"No," I said. "It wasn't that at all. It was your stupid blunder in Wiesbaden."

Stone was quiet. Too quiet. There was a movement to my left. It was Stone coming up on me.

I had started to move around the engine block, when a bright flash came from Stone's direction and a bullet ricocheted around the narrow confines of the trailer.

I threw my stiletto in the direction of the flash, but it clattered against the far wall. I had missed, and Stone laughed directly behind and above me.

In the next instance Stone had pulled me to my feet and his fists were battering my face and the side of my head. I would not be able to take much of this.

Somehow I managed to pull away from him, stumble backward over the engine block, and then spring to my feet, free of his grasp for the moment.

I was seeing bright spots and flashes of light everywhere I looked, even when I closed my eyes. And it seemed as if someone had picked up the truck and was spinning it around and around.

"The missile, Stone," I said, and then I jumped to the right and crouched down... A moment later another bright flash came from the front of the trailer, the bullet again ricocheting around inside.

I would have to get some answers from Stone. Otherwise, the president would have to be moved out of the stands.

Stone was laughing again. "I wish you would be around to see its launching."

I crept forward toward Stone's voice and then stopped. A soft scraping noise to my left alerted me, and I ducked just as something swished in the air past my head. It was all the opening I needed.

I jumped to my feet, swinging my right fist, and I connected with Stone's throat.

He let out a gasp and slammed backward against the side of the truck. An instant later he kicked me backward against the opposite wall, and I had barely time enough to drop to the floor and roll away before he started firing his gun, shot after shot, the lead ricocheting viciously around the trailer. And then it was suddenly silent.

I crawled to the back doors, the effort taking everything in my power, and through a red haze that was filling my eyes, I opened the doors and looked back.

A ricocheting bullet, shaped into a ragged piece of lead, had slammed into Stone's face just above and to the right of his nose, grinding off most of the right side of his head.

There would be no answers from him. And now in the distance I could hear the revving race-car engines as the race was about to begin. The president had received no signal from me that he was to leave, so at this moment, sure that I had solved the case, he was settling back to enjoy the race.

Earlier this morning when I had talked with him, he had agreed to leave immediately should I signal him at any time before or during the race.

I hurried around the grandstand as fast as I could go, although at times I was seeing double and my head felt as if it were about to burst open.

The president was gone. The Belgian officials were still in their seats, along with most of the Secret Service agents, but the president was no longer there.

I tried to make some sense of that. Had someone heard the commotion in the Offenbach trailer and thinking there was trouble, warned the president and made him leave?

If that was the case why hadn't the Belgian officials left? And why hadn't the other Secret Service agents gone with him? It just didn't make sense.

The race had begun just moments ago, and the cars were on the far side of the oval, so things were momentarily quiet as I headed toward the Offenbach pit. The only option left open to me now was LeMaigne himself. The president was gone, but the plot still had to be stopped, because sooner or later they would try again.

The cars had evidently been taken directly off the trucks at the Offenbach pit, because a pair of the aluminum loading ramps were still set up at trackside. I had to make my way around them as the lead cars came around the switchback curve a quarter of a mile away and headed down the long straightaway toward us.

I quickly withdrew my Luger and waited until the first Offenbach car roared past me, with LeMaigne driving. He was in fourth, and from what I could see as he flashed by, he was concentrating on his driving and not the grandstands.

Offenbach had turned around to watch the pack come by, and he noticed me standing nearby with my Luger in hand. Now he came in a dead run toward me.

I quickly holstered my gun as the man began shouting at me. "What is the matter with you?" he shouted over the roar of the race.

"It's LeMaigne." I had to shout back at him to be heard.

For a moment I was sure Offenbach was going to hit me, but then he seemed almost deflated. "LeMaigne?" he said. "What is it?"

"He's a murderer," I said. "The president of the United States is here at the race. LeMaigne and his people have already tried to assassinate him three times. They will try again sometime during the race."

Offenbach looked sharply at me. "And you are not with the Amalgamated Press?"

I shook my head, pulled out my wallet, and showed him my Secret Service identification. "We traced the organization to your plant and to LeMaigne himself. We must stop him before it's too late."

Offenbach blanched. He turned and went back into the pit area. A moment later he returned with a large chalkboard on a wooden frame. Quickly he chalked the message: 17 P-I-T S-T-O-P, and then by the brick retaining wall at the track's edge he waited for the pack to come around the track again. Seventeen was the car LeMaigne was driving.

I ducked down behind the wall, out of sight of any of the drivers in the race, and once again withdrew my Luger. On the off chance that LeMaigne did pull off the track, I would have him.

I was crouched at Offenbach's feet, and it seemed like a half an hour, although it was only a couple of minutes, before the lead machines came around the switchback and headed down the straightaway toward us. Offenbach leaned forward, holding the chalked message high over his head, and angled up the track so that the drivers could see it.

Several cars roared past us, then several more, and Offenbach put the sign down. I jumped up.

"He will come in on the next lap." Offenbach said.

Already, after only a few laps, the cars had begun to spread out, and we watched in silence as the last car flashed by us, and then again I crouched down behind the wall so that LeMaigne would not be able to see me until he pulled in.

Offenbach waited by the retaining wall, and in less than a minute the lead cars roared past us, and Offenbach swore. I jumped up.

"Goddamn him! He did not stop. He did not pull in. He ignored my instructions!"

I turned and looked toward the grandstands, where suddenly I could plainly see the president and someone who looked like his son, Stanley, taking their seats. The president was back, but LeMaigne would not know that until the next lap. And I did not think he would try anything until he was sure Magnesen was settled down at least for several minutes.

And then it struck me. LeMaigne was a part of this plot, a very big part of it, and yet he was driving—which meant the attempt would come from LeMaigne's car. Either the missile was on the car or its firing mechanism was on the car. He would have to be stopped.

I turned back to Offenbach, who was staring at me. "Flag down one of the other cars," I shouted.

Offenbach just looked at me.

"Hurry," I shouted. "Flag down one of the other cars."

Quickly Offenbach chalked the number *24* in place of the *17*, and on the next lap, after LeMaigne had passed us, he held up the sign.

When number 24 had passed, Offenbach put down the chalkboard and turned to me. "Why do you want 24 in here?" he said.

"I'm driving it," I said. I headed toward the pit shack, which looked more like a concession stand

with its counter and its CINZANO and MARTINI &
ROSSI decals.

Several of Offenbach's mechanics scattered as I
jumped over the counter and grabbed a fireproofed
suit from several hanging on nails.

Offenbach sputtered his protests as I hurriedly
dressed, but I cut him off. "LeMaigne is going to
try to kill the president in the grandstands during
the race."

"What!" Offenbach screamed.

"I don't know how," I said, zippering up the
coveralls, "but he's going to try from his car during
the race. I've got to stop him."

Offenbach was shaking his head. "You may be a
good driver, Carter or Carnahan or whatever your
name is. Maybe you are even an outstanding
amateur. But you'll never survive out there."

"I must," I shouted, as number 24 roared into
the pits and the crew busied itself refueling the
machine.

Offenbach hesitated just a moment longer, as I
headed for the machine, and then he followed me,
shouting instructions for the driver to get out immediately.

Within two minutes I was secured into the machine, had strapped on my helmet, and had popped
it into first gear.

"Keep it above eight thousand RPM," Offenbach shouted at me. I eased up on the clutch and
took off.

LeMaigne, now in third place, had flashed past
me a minute ago and there would be no hope of
catching him, so I took my time accelerating down

the straightaway. He would have to catch up to me, but in such a fashion that when he passed me I would be going at race speeds. From that moment on I would have to play it by ear, because I had absolutely no idea what I would be able to do, even with my Luger, which I had tucked under my seat belt.

Past the grandstands I was coming out of second gear. Down the hill I made it into third, and around the wide, sweeping curve that led back up the hill and into the woods, I managed fourth and then fifth at the top, at a relatively slow 190 miles per hour. At this speed LeMaigne would catch up to me by the time we reached the front straightaway.

A dozen cars passed me on the back half of the track and around the last wide curve before the switchback above the grandstands; then I suddenly saw LeMaigne's white Porsche on my tail, moving up on me incredibly fast.

I slammed the accelerator pedal to the floor, and the machine seemed to come alive, as the tachometer climbed above the ten thousand-RPM mark toward the red line.

My speed was well over 200 miles per hour when LeMaigne went by me, and then I forgot everything else except keeping behind LeMaigne and keeping alive.

The switchback was less than a half mile ahead of us, and still LeMaigne was not braking. For a few panicky moments I was sure the man was going to crash straight ahead into the hill below the restaurant, but at the last possible instant, LeMaigne's car slowed and began to slide sideways in a drift, and he flashed around the curve.

It seemed like an hour to me before I managed to get around the curve, and already LeMaigne was shifting through the gears down the straightaway, pulling away from me at an incredible speed.

Offenbach was right. I was an amateur and had no business in this race. It would almost be like a mild-mannered accountant suddenly finding himself in a Minnesota Vikings football game during the Superbowl and hoping to compete. I was simply outclassed.

I flashed by the Offenbach pit, but Offenbach was nowhere in sight. Then I was past the grandstands, and in the instant I had to look up, I could plainly see the president and his son.

Again I plunged into the race, as I came up the hill and around the wide curve, but this time I kept my foot on the floor once I had the machine in fifth gear again, and the tach climbed up to the red line and passed it. I was going faster now than the car was designed for. But there was no alternative. I would have to catch up with LeMaigne.

I eased past four cars on the back stretch, and this time I did catch up with LeMaigne just as he flashed around the switchback. I left my braking until the last instant and then lay on the pedal, the back end of the car sliding around, and somehow, miraculously, I was around the curve and heading directly behind LeMaigne.

Suddenly everything was clear to me—chillingly clear. A man in Offenbach coveralls was just running back into the pit from where he had moved the pair of aluminum loading ramps to the track's edge. LeMaigne's car was headed that way now, and I could see that if LeMaigne hit the ramps his car would be launched in a direct line to where the president was sitting.

The car itself was the missile. LeMaigne was going to launch his car off the ramps, killing himself but crashing into the president's box seat and killing everyone for two dozen rows around him.

I kept my foot to the floor, the tachometer needle completely off the scale, and less than twenty yards from the ramp, I managed to cut between LeMaigne and the ramps.

LeMaigne, seeing the danger, swerved off and flashed past the ramp down the straightaway, and I backed off on the pedal, downshifting once, twice, three times while pumping the brakes.

I had stopped him the first time, but there could not be a second, or he might be successful.

I managed to stop my car just down from the grandstands, and in a break in the pack made a U-turn on the track and slowly headed back toward the Offenbach pit.

There was not enough time to warn the president and get him out of the stands or to move the ramps. LeMaigne would be around the track in less than three minutes.

Yet I was going to have to stop him this time around, away from the crowds so that he could not hurt anyone. I was going to have to try to force him off the track and into the stone retaining wall across the track and above the pits.

On the far side of the track, across from the Offenbach pit, I stopped the car, jammed it into first gear, and sat revving the engine waiting for LeMaigne. Around me I could see several race officials and police officers running toward me, and across the track a man in coveralls was coming my way. He was carrying a gun.

My head seemed to be splitting in two again, and my vision was going double because of the concussion. I tried to focus on the man coming at me from the Offenbach pits, but I could not make out his face. I was sure, however, that he was one of the Offenbach mechanics, someone LeMaigne had arranged to hire.

I grabbed my Luger from where I had it tucked under my seat belt and fired one shot at the man but missed him. He dropped to his knees and fired a shot at me that whined off the cowling in front of the windshield. I fired again and a third time, missing both shots, as the lead car came around the switchback.

It wasn't LeMaigne, but the white Porsche could not be far behind.

If the man shooting at me had remained where he knelt he would probably have lived. I could not see well enough now to hit him with my shooting. But he was a bad shot, and he jumped up and headed for me as Offenbach came out of the pit shack and shouted at him. The man was unaware that the lead car had aimed for the space in the road between him and me.

When the Ferarri struck the man, the low body of the machine flipped him straight up into the air and backward at least two hundred feet.

I did not wait to see what happened to the Ferrari's driver as LeMaigne's car, now in second place, flashed around the switchback and I popped the clutch and slammed the accelerator pedal to the floor.

I'm sure LeMaigne did not know what was happening until it was too late. He was concentrating on lining up with the launching ramp, when at the last moment he looked up, to see me bearing down on him. At the last moment he swerved to avoid a head-on collision, and our wheels touched lightly, but hard enough to make me slide sideways.

From that point everything seemed to go in incredibly slow motion.

From my position moving sideways down the track I could see LeMaigne's car skid, then flip over once, jump straight up, come down in the middle of the track, and explode, scattering pieces of wreckage everywhere. And then I was going backward, my hands bending the steering wheel nearly off the column, and my foot jammed tightly on the brakes.

I came around again and saw the solid stone retaining wall heading my way far too fast, as several other cars skidded past me going in the opposite direction, and then I was backward again as I crashed. Then nothing.

XVI

AFTERWARDS THEY TOLD me I had been unconscious for thirty days. They had managed to pull my mangled body out of the wreck just moments before it caught fire and exploded.

I had spent five days at a hospital in Spa and another ten days in Brussels before I was moved to the Bethesda naval hospital in Maryland.

That was nearly three months ago, and today I was going to be released from AXE's rest-and-recuperation farm outside Phoenix.

I looked up from where I sat in a chaise longue by the pool as Kazuka Akiyama, stunning in her brief white bikini, came across the patio with my drink.

She had asked for and been granted an extended leave of absence from her duties at AXE's Tokyo bureau to be with me, and in that time I was sure had fallen in love with her.

"There's someone here to see you, Nicholas," she said, smiling. She handed me my drink, bent down and kissed me on the forehead, and then turned to leave.

"Don't go," I said, but she just laughed and went back into the lounge.

Three men came across the patio from the opposite side of the pool, and at first I could not make out who they were, because the sun was in my eyes. But then I recognized the voices, and started to get up.

"Don't get up, Carter," President Magnesen said, and I slumped back in the chair as he, his son Stanley, and David Hawk pulled up chairs and sat down around me.

"How are you feeling?" the president asked.

"Better," I said.

"Finally," Hawk grunted. "I've got another assignment for you."

I said nothing, but Stanley sat forward.

"Mr. Carter," he said politely, "how did you know Olanda was involved in the plot?"

I looked across at the young man, who had cut his hair so that it was just fashionably long like his father's. He was wearing new casual clothes instead of his usual uniform of tattered blue jeans and sweatshirts.

"Looks like you've copped out to the establishment," I said lightly.

Stanley seemed slightly embarrassed. "I was getting a little old to play the unwashed radical kid," he said. "There's too much to be done."

His father nodded. "As long as he doesn't go into politics."

Stanley glanced sharply at his father, and I suspected it would be a while yet before all the old wounds between them were healed.

"I didn't know Olanda was a part of it, or at least I wasn't sure until she came to my room in Frankfurt the morning of the race and tried to kill me," I said. It all seemed like it had happened so long ago.

"But you must have suspected her," Stanley insisted.

"Yes," I admitted. "Almost from the beginning, when she tried to seduce me in Tokyo," I said. "I managed to stop the assassination attempt in Honolulu, and she was sent to either discredit me with your father and get me thrown off the assignment—which she almost did—or get rid of me—which she also almost managed to do."

"And you suspected me for a while as well, didn't you?" Stanley said softly. There was another embarrassed silence.

"Yes," I said. "But I suspected almost everyone at the beginning. It's part of my job. I figured Olanda might have something to do with it, and . . ."

"I was with Olanda and against my father," Stanley finished.

"But what about Stone?" the president asked.

"Stone was a surprise and a disappointment in a

way. He was a war hero, but he was the brains behind it all. He was the only one who had the inside knowledge of your movements and habits to set it up. He was the only one with the operational experience to be able to pull it off. And evidently he had a grudge against you. That part I'm not so sure of. But I didn't know about Stone for sure until Wiesbaden. You had called me off the assignment because you were worried that your son was somehow involved and would be found out. But although you knew I was in Wiesbaden, I knew you would never send your head Secret Service man after me. You might have called Hawk and asked him to send someone, but you wouldn't have sent Stone."

"True," the president said. "Stone was supposed to be on his way to Spa to check on the final security arrangements for the race, but he told me he went through Wiesbaden and by coincidence happened to see you on the street and followed you. I was too confused about everything myself to even entertain the slightest suspicions for the moment."

"Stone rescued me to throw me off his trail," I said. "Besides, he wanted me around in case you thought about backing out of going to the race. I was the only one you were listening to. And in addition, he still had not figured out who I really was—one mystery he didn't care for."

Magnesen glanced at his son and then back at me. "We let Stanley in on your real identity because he already suspected too much. You just didn't act like a Secret Service agent."

I sat forward and lit myself a cigarette, still a bit

dissatisfied because the assignment wasn't completely done.

"You've done a fine job, Carter," the president was saying, but I shook my head.

"I didn't find out why they wanted you dead," I said.

"That's easy, or relatively easy," Magnesen said, and nodded toward Hawk. "Your boss dug a little deeper into Stone's background these past few weeks, and he found out that Stone was mentally unbalanced. It evidently happened because of the war. But the single psychological evaluation form on him somehow got misplaced from his records. I'm sure that since Stone was in military intelligence, he didn't find it very difficult to alter his records. At that time he had no plot in mind; he just saw the negative psychological report as a deterrent to his military career."

"But why kill you during the world tour?" I asked. "And what did Inge Torman mean when she said your assassination and the three attempts that were meant to fail were nothing but an exercise?"

"Megalomania," Stanley said. "I studied that in school."

"That and an American missile base in Portugal," the president continued. "Our plans evidently leaked to the wrong people. Stone had intelligence contacts all over the world, and he found out about the missile-base plans and Inge Torman's plans to assassinate me during my world tour, and he simply took over."

"It was a Portugese plot from the beginning?" I asked.

The president nodded. "At the beginning it was. Inge Torman, who was in the same terrorist group as Juan Portenjo, had planned my assassination as early as six months ago. But when Stone got wind of what was going on, he took charge. It was a tailor-made organization for him. He added the Japanese, the Arab, and the German elements to it. Stone believed he was invincible; that's why he played at killing me the first three times. He wanted to prove how good he was."

"And LeMaigne?" I asked.

"Hawk found out that Inge Torman was LeMaigne's wife. They were both members of the Communist party. Both had been trained in Moscow. With his wife dead, he had nothing to live for. Also a part of Stone's plan, to make sure LeMaigne did not back out at the last moment."

Hawk had risen, and now the president and his son got up. I got to my feet as well and shook hands with them.

"Thanks again for a job well done," Magnesen said.

"Yes, sir," I said.

"I'll see you in my office in the morning," Hawk growled, but I shook my head.

"Not until Monday," I said. "There's a little unfinished business I have to attend to first."

I headed toward the lounge and Kazuka Akiyama.